I0521326

Lyra's last conscious thought was being trapped under debris in a dam collapse. When her consciousness woke up, things were . . . different.

She was in her sixth decade, but her body was slight and curvy, and she had a lot of blue hair in lieu of her normal mud brown. That was different.

She meets the medical team, and they are aliens with pointy ears. Fair enough. She now has pointy ears as well.

A briefing lets her know she is an omega. She is the only omega on the entire planet and the first of her kind to wake. What follows is a dizzying culture shock, a lot of firsts, and being the target of a mate-drive run that will see her with partners by the end of it. The first Omega Run since the natural omegas died. What could go wrong?

The unauthorized reproduction or distribution of this copyrighted work is illegal. Criminal copyright infringement, including infringement without monetary gain, is investigated by the FBI and is punishable by up to 5 years in federal prison and a fine of $250,000.

This book is a work of fiction. Names, characters, places, and incidents either are products of the author's imagination or are used fictitiously. Any resemblance to actual events or locales or persons, living or dead, is entirely coincidental.

Omega Run
Copyright © 2023 Viola Grace and Taryn Jameson
ISBN: 978-1-4874-3972-9
Cover art by Angela Waters

All rights reserved. Except for use in any review, the reproduction or utilization of this work in whole or in part in any form by any electronic, mechanical or other means, now known or hereafter invented, is forbidden without the written permission of the publisher.

Published by eXtasy Books Inc

Look for us online at:
www.eXtasybooks.com

Omega Run
Recycled Souls, Book 1

By

Viola Grace and Taryn Jameson

CHAPTER ONE

Pulling air into her lungs was the hardest thing she had ever done, but Lyra managed it. The heavy wheeze of her breath was the only sound in her room, but as she rolled to her side, she heard a shrill beeping.

This was wrong. Everything was wrong.

She was wearing a white gown of soft fabric and knew she didn't own anything like it. She favoured T-shirts or nothing.

A woman in a version of a medical tunic and skirt came into the room via a silvery door. She stared for a moment, and Lyra stared back. The woman concisely said, "Oh!" and backed out of the room, closing the door.

Lyra pushed to a sitting position and rubbed her hand, blinking at the texture. Her skin felt weird, like super soft, and the scars that she was used to weren't there. The nails were neatly trimmed and not like her bitten fingertips.

She pulled her hair around and stared at the navy blue. *Oh shit. This isn't me. Who the hell am I?*

The door opened again, and a man in medical clothing was with the woman. "By the stars, it worked."

Lyra looked at them and swung her legs off the bed. She slowly stood and stared at the two beings who where decidedly larger than she.

She swayed, and her feet felt the cold radiating from the floor. She licked her lips. "Who are you, and why am I in this body? I don't belong here."

The woman folded her hands together. "Where do you think you belong?"

"I was drowning. Dying. I couldn't breathe. The floodwater had me, and I was tangled in debris. The world got dark, and then I woke up here. The problem is, this isn't my body." The

1

words tumbled as she had in the floodwaters.

The medical team looked at each other. The woman said, "What do you mean?"

"I mean, this isn't my body. How tall are you?"

The woman frowned. "Average height."

"What species are you?" She looked at the other two, and they were vaguely human but had silvery skin, dark lines around their eyes, and ears that were pointed and nearly elfin.

They looked at each other, and the female went to a cupboard and brought a mirror out. "We are the same species that you are, miss. Now, what is your name?"

She stared into a mirror where her blue hair, violet eyes, and pearlescent skin were not what she remembered having. Her ears were pointed, and her lips were blushing pink. She was pretty. *Damn.* "This isn't my face."

Lyra didn't know what they were supposed to do or say, but it wasn't her face. It wasn't her body. She had been a grey person. Unremarkable in every way—brown hair, brown eyes and skin that spoke to her muddled genetics. Her body had been straight, and this new one had curves everywhere she looked, but she needed to know what to do when the original owner came back.

"Who do you think I am?" she challenged.

The male smiled slightly. "Omega Yten."

She frowned. Omega had an identifying sense to it, and Yten was a number. Three.

"That isn't a name."

The woman inclined her head. "We are depending on you to provide your name."

"Lyra. What do the other identifiers mean?"

"You are an omega and the third attempt to renew your designation in our population."

"Designation?"

The male smiled. "Let us do health checks and scan your brain output."

"Will it hurt?"

He shook his head. "No. You are a precious output of the project. Injury is the last thing we want."

The female said, "We have an informative film for you to watch."

"Oh, goody." She took a few steps on the floor. "So, let's get this party started."

"You aren't going go object or fight?"

Lyra shrugged. "I was dead. I know I was dead. I don't know who was supposed to be in this body, but if they come back, I will leave . . . somehow."

The woman took her hand and led her out of the silvery door into a hallway. There was a clatter of an instrument tray when Lyra entered an exam chamber. Medical staff were staring at her.

"Excuse me, miss. Why are they staring at me?"

The woman smiled. "When you see the video, you will understand."

"Oh. Okay."

"You have strange speech patterns."

"Well, based on the pointy ears, my soul is in the wrong body."

The medical staff were listening keenly; their silvery skin was very definitely not human.

They led her to a bed, and the female lifted her dress over her head before helping her hop up and settling her in place. She placed a halo with a clear gem on the forehead on Lyra's head and ordered to relax.

She pursed her lips. There was nothing like being ordered to relax to make sure that it never happened.

Her temples tingled where the halo pressed against her skin, and a crimson light filled the room.

All of the physicians were silent until the tingle stopped and the light winked out.

Lyra asked, "What was that?"

The male who had been in her room said, "It was a species identifier. It denoted your origin."

"Oh. Great."

The female snickered.

The rest of the scans went along without any discomfort, and then the female murmured, "Breathe deep. This is the final exam."

Soft loops snagged her wrists and held her down, her ankles were treated to the same, and then they were widened. The probe that pressed against her sex and slipped inside made her squirm. When the probe began to swell, her eyes got huge, and she tried to move again. They released a mist near her face, and the thick scent made her cough, but there was a flood of moisture from between her thighs that would dehydrate her if it continued. It was an exaggeration, but it was disconcerting. The scent faded, and the probe pulled free of her without deflating.

She gasped and heard a sound from her throat that she had never heard before. A soft whine that was desperate and begging.

She shuddered, and the cuffs released. Lyra slammed her legs together and sat up. "What the actual fuck was that?"

The medics stared in shock at her attitude.

The male she had met was looking at her in dawning glee. "We have a successful omega!"

"Shall I alert the project heads?" The female grinned.

"At once. They are going to want to meet her."

Lyra made a T with her hands. "Time out. I need clothes and a towel. I don't know what was in that probe, but I am soaked."

She looked down at her breasts with nipples the same pale pink as her lips and the neatly trimmed thatch of blue pubic hair. "Yeah, clothes are good."

The male said, "I will clothe her; you send the missive. I expect to have a representative down here within the hour."

They nodded to each other, and the physician, whom she now suspected was a researcher, stared. She knew nerd face when she saw it. He was examining her coldly. She was a project. He had said as much. He carefully helped her off the table and showed her where to go. There was a changing area where there were slippers and a rack of gowns. They were way too fancy to be dresses.

He handed her a gold gown, and she scowled. "No. Wrong colour."

She flipped through the dresses, found a gown with white layers, checked it for opacity, then slipped it over her head, tucking her breasts into the empire bodice.

"I thought it would wash out your skin, but it is striking."

She flapped the long and wide sleeves. "I just had to check it wasn't see-through. Now, where is the video that explains things . . . and where's my towel?"

He was laughing and handed her a cloth. She hiked up the floor-length skirt and got rid of the excessive moisture, folding the cloth with the residue inside. He took it and smiled. "Thank you, Omega Yten Lyra."

She blinked. "You're welcome?"

He grinned. "Come; I will show you to the gallery where you can see why you are here."

Lyra nodded and wiggled her toes in the slippers. "Why are all the clothes my size?"

"Because all the omegas that we generated were from the same body blanks."

"So, there wasn't anyone in this body before me?"

He shook his head. "No."

She was relieved, but as they walked through the halls, part of her was also terrified. How had she gotten into a body that definitely was not hers?

The gallery had a seat in the centre of it. Paintings of pointy-eared warriors were everywhere, and the chair was aimed at a blank space. When she sat and settled in, the projection began with a history lesson, and she learned where she was and why she was there.

She was a sex toy for a specific part of the population.

Lyra watched the History of the MaKorith. Three classes of beings made up their society. Alphas, betas, and omegas. The betas were the most plentiful, the alphas were the warriors and tacticians, and the omegas . . . they kept the alphas calm.

A beta uprising wiped out the omegas, and some folk thought that it would give their society a reason to banish the alphas to some other worlds, but the alphas cracked down, took betas as mates, and with every generation, there were fewer of the golden ones who kept the MaKorith thriving.

The Su'ath were the catalyst for the change in attitude. The shapeshifting race began attacking outposts, and the betas ran to the alphas for help. They agreed if the betas could bring omegas back.

The scientists combined alien tech from a dozen worlds, and the omega project was underway, but transferring consciousness wasn't possible, so they had to use dimensional gateways to pull suitable souls through and coax them into the vessels.

When a consciousness settled, a transformation began, and the blank took on unmistakable aspects of life.

The description of omegas was lacklustre. It just described them as soft in body and speech, delicate, and made to be protected and doted on by alphas. Only omegas could soothe them and let them become stronger beyond their alpha tempers and riotous emotions. *Delightful.*

There was a physical scale of the MaKorith, and she blinked. "No fucking way."

Omegas were six inches smaller than betas, who were twelve inches smaller than alphas. The alphas were nearly seven feet tall, and she was five feet if she were lucky. That wasn't a size differential she had ever attempted, but she had been a tall woman. A tall, unremarkable woman. Now she was a tiny, pale, blue-haired, and purple-eyed woman with boobs that were double what her hands could manage and an exaggerated hourglass for a figure. It was the type of body she used to dream of having, but now, it freaked her out. Designed to be prey.

She was staring at the blank space when there was a growl from behind her. "You are the right size, but are you a true omega?"

She turned and saw the researcher standing next to a huge creature with golden skin, long black hair pulled back in a bound ponytail, and pointed ears. His glittering green eyes were huge and outlined with black.

"What the fuck is that?" She screamed and moved into the gallery, hiding behind a pillar with a statue on it.

The man who had spoken paused, and his lips twisted in a smile. The researcher looked nervous. "I will retrieve her."

"No. Let me." The man was dressed in a black military uniform that made him look even bigger, not that it was necessary.

She hid behind the pillar as the giant came for her. When he got close, she darted to the next pillar, and he snickered. Then, when he got close again, she gauged his speed and dove between his legs, sliding and scrambling to her feet on the other side. He was laughing as he turned to grab her, and the moment he got near her and she prepared to bolt, his arms snapped forward, and he caught her, lifting her off her feet.

"That was interesting. You have an instinct to run. Good. There hasn't been an Omega Run in centuries. I think it would be a good way to introduce you to your alphas. It will also separate the weak from the determined."

She kicked at him, and he held her out of range. "Don't you mean the strong?"

He laughed. "We are all strong, but some are content with a beta in their bed. Those who want an omega will line up and fight for the honour to become yours."

She frowned. "Alphas used to possess the omegas."

"Yes, but now there is only one of you, so belonging to the omega is a badge of honour for the males."

"Why are you speaking in plural?" She caught his scent, and it teased at her, but something in that masculine scent made her frown. He wasn't for her.

He looked at her and narrowed his gaze.

"Well, you aren't for me, so it doesn't matter. Put me down."

He grinned and gently set her on her feet. "Your accent is strange, and your reflexes are not the soft and quiet ones of the ancient omegas, so you are something new, but I don't want to expose you to a rutting alpha unless we can find one guaranteed to be both sufficiently ranking and acceptable to you."

She wrinkled her nose. "Bring me an article of clothing from each of them. A glove, a shirt. Whatever. I seem to be mostly scent-triggered."

"Who were you, little omega?"

She looked up at him and scowled. "That is disturbingly accurate. I was Lyra Omanic. I worked at a dam that collapsed and flooded the area it was designed to keep dry. I was trapped in debris and being pulled under, and then I woke up here."

The guy crouched slowly. "You have been in that body for four months. That is when the brain activity indicator lit up, and you started to gain pigmentation. You designed yourself."

She frowned. "Really? The blue hair is a little odd."

He chuckled. "We thought so, too, but you were given instruction that you could change the pigment and nothing else."

"You have a mate, right?" She cocked her head.

He nodded. "I do. You can tell?"

She nodded. "There is a scent that I translate as bitter, so I was guessing what it meant."

Lyra was standing with her hands in front of her and talking to a giant that could have been made of three of her. "So, do the alphas just appear randomly in the population?"

He nodded. "We do. Fifteen out of a hundred are alphas. Five percent used to be omegas, but gene therapy destroyed all of your kind. Omegas have weak immune systems on their own, and the younger ones failed while the mated ones sickened and died after exposure to the virus. The alphas withdrew from their positions as leaders and warriors and let the betas have the world. We expelled anyone who wasn't a mate from one of the southern continents, and we left the betas to live the life they wanted to lead. It took thirty-five years, but they begged for the alphas to return to assist and guide them when they were threatened by the Su'ath. We let them suffer for a few years before we returned and activated all the old equipment designed for us." He chuckled. "Of course, there was a deal to be made, so we negotiated for a return of the omegas with a sturdier biology."

She blinked. "So, alien tech and blank bodies and then the betas baited for souls. When they caught one, they moved me into an incubator. Right now, I have an image of a bunch of bodies on slabs at the top of the building with a magnifying lens firing at them."

"It is a bit more of an orb in a dimensional rift. There is a video of the transfer moment if you want to see it." He stood and offered his hand.

"Well, since I am not attracted to you, this is not going to lead to any kind of weird orgy, so I will say sure."

"You are certain of that?"

"Well, I am pretty sure. You are alone, and you seem to have a rank insignia that I don't quite understand, and I am all teeny and weak, so I can just faint my way out of stuff, and most of the time, guys like you will have to wake me up before making a move."

"You have an interesting view on the situation. Why would we wait before taking advantage?"

She smiled brightly. "Because I am the only working prototype you have. If I start screaming every time someone touches me, you won't be able to show me to other folks as a successful return of the omegas." She looked at him and let her inner terror at what was going on show in her expression.

He frowned, and a caring expression took over his face. "It's okay. Come here."

She took two steps toward him, and he picked her up and hugged her. She snickered. "Sucker."

He looked at her in surprise. "You . . . were not feeling afraid?"

"No. Well, yes and no. I am terrified. I am not whatever species you are, you are way bigger than me, and I don't know where I am and what's going to happen next, but in my previous life, I was working maintenance in a dam with millions of tons of water over my head at any given time. You get used to working and ignoring the fear. I mean, sex in that situation would be weird. I might let the control slip for a bit if there was a guy I wasn't fond of coming at me and cry a little."

He looked at her and laughed. "Huh. You are a complicated creature. Come with me. You need to learn about our world far beyond our designations. I will introduce you to my wife, and you can discuss things with her."

He started walking away with her, and the researcher stumbled beside them. "Sir . . . uh . . . Your Highness, you can't take her out of the facility."

The man holding her turned and grinned down at the researcher. "Why can't I?"

"We have tests to run."

"You ran your tests today. She is coming with me and will reside at my home with all the guards that are necessary."

"You can't have her guarded by alphas. When her scent comes in, they will be thrown into rut. If she goes into heat before things get organized, there will be chaos."

The president smiled and settled her on the crook of his arm, which made her higher than his head. "Himyana is pregnant. Her scent will keep Omega Yten Lyra calm."

He looked at the researcher. "You may come and check on her every two days. She needs to learn about our society, and that is best done with actual citizens." He chuckled. "When there are enough possible mates that she approves of, we will arrange an Omega Run, and from there, we will determine the first two that will have her as a mate."

Lyra listened to their discussion, and she was simply carried out of the facility, tucked into an armoured vehicle with the president, and it floated loose of its mooring and headed toward the city far below.

"Don't worry, Yten Lyra. You are safe."

She looked around with wide eyes at their path and the sky around them. "People are flying!"

"Of course. How do you think we can tell who is an alpha? They develop skills beyond that of betas, and the bodies finish evolving later."

She looked at him and said, "Why don't you sign me up for the same social studies and history you would give a child beginning education? I am learning how a world works, and working it from what I see to try and guess at the origins is just going to make me make mistakes."

The president smiled. "So, the idea of the additional talents is not unfamiliar to you."

"They were the stuff of fiction and entertainment." Lyra

realized her speech patterns were changing.

He laughed. "Perhaps that is what drew your consciousness here."

She sat up on her knees and looked out the window at the city filled with ground transport and tiny betas walking from building to building. If it weren't for the skin tones, people flying, and vehicles flying, it could be any city on Earth.

Lyra looked over at the man who was catching up on correspondence on a tablet, his gold skin and pointed ears. This definitely wasn't Earth. So, what was going to happen to her now?

CHAPTER TWO

The transport landed in a large garden, and a guard stepped forward to open the door. The president got out ahead of her and then turned back to beckon to her. "You are safe here, Yten Lyra."

"Why keep the Yten ahead of my name?"

"Your entire generation is known as Yten. The previous attempts were Ytall and Ywon. Neither of those batches had a successful omega. I wanted to get you away from the researchers so that they didn't test you until you were destroyed."

She swallowed and scooted toward him. "How long am I staying here?"

"Until you are in heat or until the alphas know you exist. Once that happens, there will be a pile here at the residence. They will gather and fight for the chance to meet you."

She stepped out of the vehicle but didn't touch him. He raised his brows.

"You have a mate, and mates get funny about the scent of another woman on their male. Pregnant women have keen senses."

"I have already carried you."

"Ah, right. But my skin hasn't been in contact with your skin aside from your hands, so wash up."

He laughed. "It is funny that you are giving me orders. I believe I understand the allure of omegas. Everything you do is adorable."

She grimaced. "I suppose that is something I need to get used to. I have never been considered cute."

He snorted. "Come with me, and meet my wife. You will soon know how you are considered. Himyana does not pull her punches."

They walked across lush bluish grass, and she walked next to him with her hands together. The guards were stern, but they did double-takes when they saw her.

A woman with golden hair, an excited expression, and a belly that looked eight months along came out of the building.

"Is that her?" The woman laughed and smiled. "She's so tiny."

The first lady was five-eight and further along when she turned sideways. She had a really good seamstress.

The president kissed his wife, and watching it made Lyra's eyes widen. That wasn't a chaste peck on the lips. He was checking her tonsils, and she was returning the favour.

His wife was limp in his arms when he lifted his head. She exhaled. "Ah. Right. Missed you, too."

He grinned. "Himyana, high lady of the MaKorith, this is Omega Yten Lyra."

Lyra curtsied. "Pleased to meet you, Lady."

Himyana looked her over, and the president closed the doors they had walked through while he had been kissing his pregnant wife.

Lyra stood still as the woman walked around her.

"You are adorable. May I hug you?"

"Sure." Lyra stood still while the much taller woman hugged her, and her nose was near the lady's collarbone. The swell of the belly was kicking.

Himyana hummed happily and rubbed her hands over Lyra's back and up to her neck. She moved her cheek against Lyra's, and the humming turned to soft sighs. "You feel so good. Your skin is so soft."

"The baby seems healthy."

Himyana lifted her head. "Hm? Yes. Very. It will be in my arms in four weeks or less."

Lyra blinked, and the woman kept stroking her cheeks.

"Okay, I can see why alphas were pissed when omegas were destroyed. If I had you with me, I would cuddle up with you every night."

Lyra blinked again and cocked her head. "I knew I was some kind of doll."

The president laughed.

Himyana sighed. "Imko. You didn't tell her that, did you?"

"No. She is learning from the situations around her and guessing at her position."

The woman looked around. "You didn't bring clothing for her?"

Lyra sighed. "Nope. He picked me up like a toy and hauled me through the facility. You will probably have to send in a request for more clothing for me."

Himyana waved that away. "I have a seamstress in the building. She will be delighted to work on you."

"Uh, how long am I going to be here?"

The lady grinned. "Until some of the alphas believe we actually have a working omega."

"Am I a living thing or some kind of robot?" Lyra looked at her hands.

The two looked at each other, and they frowned. The president said, "You are a living entity. The blank they used was based on a genetic sample from a female omega. If you have all the reproductive function that the scans indicate you have, you should have a normal omega life."

Himyana grinned. "Right down to the marking and mating."

"Marking? Mating?"

Himyana's eyes widened. "Oh. Right. You might not have that. I will explain."

"Lyra has suggested that we make all educational and historical materials available, as we would to a child."

A knock on the door preceded the entry of three alphas with tablets and scowls. They froze in place when they saw Lyra.

"Mr. President, is that . . ." a heavily muscled blonde asked.

Lyra walked up to the men, put her hand on her hips, looked up at them, and said, "Boo!"

Himyana laughed and quickly put her arm around Lyra, ushering her out of the room and down the hall. "That was really dangerous, Yten Lyra."

"Just Lyra, Lady."

"Himmy. Call me Himmy."

"Himmy, why are you rushing me out of the room and down this hallway?"

"Because those three were unattached alphas, and they might not be content with a light touch or a hug. They aren't the ones that Imko wants for you."

"So, he is using me for political gain?"

"Absolutely. You are being used to cement a team, and if any of the others wake, they are going to be used the same way."

Lyra sighed as she was pushed along by the very sprightly pregnant lady. They turned into a room that looked like a fancy living space, and Himmy closed the door behind them.

"I am going to order some refreshments. When did you last eat?"

Lyra looked around the room decorated with a lot of weaponry on the walls. "Um, I don't know. They haven't fed me yet, so I don't know what I like."

"Oh, this is going to be fun. I am going to order some of everything."

Lyra looked at her, and the woman had her fingers pressed to her ear, and she was talking rapidly using terms that seemed food related. When Himmy finished, she smiled happily. "I have been hoping for an excuse to do that. Imko has been watching my intake carefully in the hope that I won't get much bigger. My belly is his favourite feature, but it's freaking him out a bit."

"So, is this your first?" Lyra smiled at her.

Himmy paused and said, "It will be our only child. I can't physically carry a second child from an alpha. That is one of the reasons that we are desperate for omegas. Not every alpha can find a suitable mate, and the random births don't keep the population stable."

"Why were the omegas killed?" Lyra asked calmly. "It seems like the thing folks like me should know."

"Let's wait for the tea and snacks. This is a long conversation."

Lyra nodded. "Why all the weapons?"

"Ah, they are mine. A lot of them are captured Su'ath

weapons."

Lyra looked at the woman who bent at the knees to pick up a tablet from a table. "Can I help you?"

Himmy smiled. "If you could help me sit, that would be great."

Lyra moved over to her side and helped her descend onto the couch. "I even promise to help you up again later."

Himmy blinked and laughed. "You have been around pregnant women before."

"I had sisters. Three older sisters. They all had kids. I had twelve nieces and nephews." Lyra plumped a pillow and tucked it behind Himmy.

Himmy blinked. "That many?"

"Sure. I have seven siblings myself. Had. Different world, different body."

She made sure that Himmy was settled and walked back to the wall of weapons. There were axes, compressed cylinders, daggers. "These were all taken off fallen warriors, right?"

"Yeah, how can you tell?"

"They are all for close combat."

"I was a peacekeeper on Peltin before the alphas returned to us. That is how I met Imko." Himmy chuckled. "I was being held in a Su'ath warship, and they came to rescue us when the Ywon omegas had been generated. I am glad for it, but having grown up with only the tales of alphas, it was startling to see a group of them in the flesh."

"But you had seen alphas before, right? You are the same species."

"We are, and we are not. They have genetics activated that betas don't have. We carry them, but they don't become apparent."

"But the omega genes were wiped out of the population."

"Correct. You are the first living omega anyone has seen walking around in decades. Those that passed had genetic samples taken, and it was one of those dead omegas that your body is modelled on, and her genes are in your body."

Lyra reached out to touch one of the cylinders, and at her touch, it lit up, and swirling patterns covered the metal. She pulled her hand back quickly and went to sit with Himmy. "So, where did the body blanks come from?"

"Imko won't tell me. The citizens at large were just told that alien tech was being used to return omegas to our population. I don't know if you will ever know precisely how you got here."

"What happened to the other two generations?"

"Something was wrong with them. They only lived a few days and never left the facility." Himmy sighed. "They didn't even report consciousness according to the researchers."

There was a soft knock, and Himmy called out for the person to come in. A beta woman with a smile in a sober uniform brought a tray in. "You ordered a lot, Lady."

Himmy smirked. "I have a guest. Hence the extra teacup."

The servant looked up as she set the tray down, and it dropped the last quarter inch with a clatter. Himmy jumped, and Lyra grinned and waved. "Hello, miss."

"You're a . . ."

Lyra shrugged. "That's what they say. I don't see it myself. I think I just need a tan." She held out her hand with its pearl skin.

Himmy snorted. "Thank you, Mabella."

The maid or whatever was frozen, staring at Lyra.

Himmy chuckled. "You can go now, Mabella. Yten Lyra will help me if I need it."

Mabella blinked and stood up straight. "Yes, Lady."

The stunned servant left the room, and Lyra went to pour tea as her grandma had taught her. The cups were smooth with no handles.

"How thermally resistant are the cups?"

"Very. Pour them two-thirds full, and we hold the cup from the top. That's why the cup is flared. It also keeps the heat in." She took the teacup from Lyra, held it by the rim, and sipped before setting the cup down. "Like that."

Lyra nodded and sipped at the tea. "That's really good."

"Try the purple sandwiches. They are my favourite."

Lyra took one of the sandwiches and looked at Himmy. "What can I get for you?"

Himmy smiled, pointed, and described all the sandwiches

and treats she wanted. Himmy urged Lyra to try one of every-thing, and they chortled and giggled their way through the snacks. Lyra learned a lot about the food and flavours that the MaKorith enjoyed, or at least the ones that Himmy enjoyed.

They were nearly through the snacks when the president came in and surveyed the devastation on the tray. "Huh. Himyana, have you been stuffing yourself again?" He leaned over and kissed her. "That's my job."

Lyra chuckled. According to Himmy, Imko was more overtly sexual than most, but his skills as an alpha were phys-ical, so he liked to touch and be touched. Fortunately, Himmy responded to him excitedly, and it was what he needed.

There were betas out there who could take on an alpha, but they were few and far between. The Su'ath seemed to collect that kind of beta as well, but once they were captured, they were rarely recovered.

Lyra waited until Imko finished kissing his mate and sipped at her tea while she watched. When the kiss was over, Imko was on the couch and his wife was in his lap.

He sighed happily with one hand on the huge swell of Himmy's belly. Lyra smiled.

Imko asked, "So, did you feel anything when you watched us?"

"Not particularly. I think you are cute together. Why?"

Imko sighed. "Just wondering if your hormones have kicked in yet."

"Nope. All I can confirm is that I don't want to have sex with either one of you."

Himmy grimaced. "That is unfortunate."

Imko sighed. "She is aroused eighty percent of the time lately. It would have been nice to have someone who could keep her busy while I was working."

Himmy made a fist and punched him. "It's your fault, so just deal with it. You caused it; you have to fix it."

He chuckled and lifted her fist to kiss her knuckles. "I will, as soon as we aren't under surveillance."

Himmy exhaled. "I don't care."

Lyra chuckled and sipped her tea. "Go nuts; it won't

damage me. I am working through my own stuff."

Himyana laughed. "I can wait."

"You can just send me to my room. Wait. Do I have a room, or am I going back to the research centre?"

They both looked at her. "No!"

Imko sighed. "You will remain here, get acclimated to our society, and the alphas are already spreading the news that you have been sighted. Your walking up to them and saying *boo* was recorded on our cameras and is being sent to some of the more distant outposts so that they have a chance to come back here before the Omega Run is over."

Lyra cocked her head. "What is the Omega Run?"

Imko sighed. "We assemble one hundred alphas. You will scent along them to determine which ones you will not accept. We then have the remaining males compete for five days, and on the final day, you take a backpack full of markers into a reserve and hide them along the course. Each alpha has five minutes to gather as many of the markers as he can. The one with the greatest collection will be your first mate, the next one will be your second, and then a possible third can be added to your bed. At that point, their skills will be analyzed, and you and they will be assigned to an outpost to test the theory that an omega makes a team stronger."

Lyra blinked. "Three?"

Himmy frowned. "Is that a problem?"

"My species generally pair bonds. Anything outside of that is considered deviant behaviour by the masses. This is going to take some getting used to."

Imko cocked his head. "But you don't have an objection to the contest? Some species do."

Lyra shrugged. "Women and men have courtships that are defined by their circumstances and social structure. You guys have the added details of alphas, betas, and omegas in the mix. It just adds layers to the needed rituals for courtship."

Imko looked at Himmy and smiled. "What was our ritual?"

Himmy chuckled. "You broke the manacles holding me, kissed me, and told the elders that they weren't getting back to Peltin until they agreed to surrender me as payment."

Lyra giggled. "Seriously?"

Imko sighed. "Seriously. She was at the end of her receptivity, but her scent still pulled me to her. One trace of her, and I followed her scent through a warship and into the hold."

"He punched right through the wall." Himyana leaned against his shoulder.

"That is so sweet." Lyra smiled. "So, Imko, how did you end up president?"

He sighed. "I was voted in once Himyana caught."

"Caught what?"

Himyana patted her belly. "This. Only a breeding alpha can be president."

Imko sighed. "It is when alphas are considered to be most stable and forward-thinking instead of reactive."

Lyra smiled. "Probably smart."

Himmy smiled. "We will give you some vids of alphas in combat training later."

"Why?"

Himmy grinned. "If there is anything that's going to kick-start a hormonal response, it is watching half-naked alphas wrestling and fighting each other."

Imko sighed. "Down, girl. Your scent is heating up."

Lyra smirked. "If you want some alone time, you can stow me in a cupboard or something. I am travel-sized for your convenience."

Himmy laughed. "I am not that bad off. He is, but I am not."

"Well, on my world, it is pretty much the same in relationships. The ladies choose the timing unless the male is persuasive. Or in my dimension. Whatever. I really want to figure out where I came from in the grand scheme of things."

Imko frowned. "I am wondering about that as well. The other blanks have taken on different hair colours. Eye colour is uncertain. The colours are not what we would consider standard, but they are growing on the scalp, eyebrows, and groin."

"I am guessing that it indicates that there are very different people percolating under that hair." She picked up a lock of her dark-blue hair. "I drowned in water this colour."

Himmy frowned. "And that just killed my frisky impulses."

Lyra settled on a chair and said, "Sorry. It's been a busy day, and things are a little wavy."

Himyana sat up. "How are you feeling?"

"Um, hungry again. Sorry."

Imko scowled. "We are going to need the researcher here with all the historical data for the other blank projects."

"Right." Himyana grabbed her tablet and started to tap. "Those buggers should be having panic attacks by now."

Lyra leaned forward and finished off all the food and tea. "I am obnoxiously hungry."

Imko nodded. "Fair enough. Himmy, order some more food. If your body is telling you it is hungry, it is for a good reason."

She sat, and her stomach rumbled. "So, those weapons are all Su'ath?"

Imko nodded. "Himmy got them all in battle or after battles."

Himmy kicked her feet, and Imko helped her sit on the couch next to him. She started to squirm forward, and Lyra moved to help her up.

"Su'ath weapons are all very usable by anyone who picks them up, but only the warriors can charge them up."

Himmy linked arms with her and walked her to the wall with the seven weapons mounted to it. "I got all of these in the siege of Peltin. The only one I didn't see in action was the cylinder."

"I think I know where they got my body blank, and I know it is going to cause an issue." Lyra smiled.

Imko stood behind them and said, "Where?"

Omega Yten Lyra reached out and touched the cylinder that lit up, and as her fingers curled around it, the unit hummed. Metal shot out forward and back, and she stood with a spear in her hand, shrugging at the two shocked MaKorith.

The look in Imko's eyes wasn't good.

Lyra shrank the cylinder again and put it back on the wall. "Well, I guess you know what it does now. So, when the researchers get here, are they going to take me apart?"

Himmy blinked. "You are a Su'ath blank."

Imko murmured, "Just us on that front now. No one else needs to know. How did you figure it out?"

"Himmy showed me the weapons, and they started to warm up, and the cylinder glowed." Lyra stepped away from the wall of weapons to ease her hosts' battle-ready bodies. "So, what do the Su'ath look like?"

Imko blinked. "Like us, but the skin shades are tinged with red. They have been stealing citizens for the last four decades."

"Did you used to have a political relationship with the Su'ath?"

Imko frowned. "Of course. They were unstable allies."

"So, when the omegas here were killed, did theirs survive? They had them, right?"

Imko blinked. "They did not mention them, and none were ever brought to territory negotiations."

"So, you and they are not friendly . . . like ever."

Himyana shrugged. "Never. We have not exchanged personnel, and the embassies on the colony worlds have been destroyed. There is no more shared occupancy on any of our worlds."

Lyra twisted her lips and paused as two large trays were brought in. When they were alone again, she wandered over to the trays and started eating.

Imko muttered, "We are having dinner in three hours."

Lyra's stomach rumbled alarmingly, and she kept eating. "Whatever my body is doing with the food, it is doing it fast, and there doesn't seem to be any indicators of processing."

Himmy chuckled and said, "Speaking of, excuse me." She waddled her way to a door in the corner of the room.

Imko looked at Lyra. "So, do you think you are a plant of some kind?"

She met his gaze and crossed her arms. "I think the Su'ath were trying to do the same thing you are, but your guys managed to catch the consciousnesses and stuff them in the bodies. What I want to know is how this body processes food because it doesn't feel normal."

He looked at her and nodded. "Right. I am going to make

some calls. Are you up for some invasive exams?"

"Oh, baby. Talk dirty to me," she muttered.

His raised brows and grin made her realize what she had said to this guy who was nearly four times her size. She clapped a hand over her mouth.

He picked up a tablet and opened a link. "Kresso, I have a guest here who needs a full and discreet exam."

"*Has Himyana cut you off?*"

"No, if she cut me off, it would be an emergency, and you would need to bring blood." Imko chuckled. "It is for a friend of Himmy's who isn't feeling like herself."

"*Fine. I will be there in an hour. Please have me cleared for arrival.*"

"Are you sure? It is so much more fun when you fight your way in." Imko chuckled.

"*Why couldn't I have had a brother who was less political?*"

"Because then you wouldn't have a brother who was so good-looking," Imko smirked. "See you in an hour. Bring a full kit."

"*Kthack,*" the man on the screen muttered. He disappeared.

Lyra blinked at the word that didn't translate into anything other than *deviant ass fucker*. It was concise. It also meant that there was a standard method of doing it.

Imko laughed and set the tablet down. "Nice to have a physician in the family. I wonder what he is going to make of you."

Himmy came back looking relieved. "Did I hear Kresso?"

"Yeah, I called him to help with Lyra. At least I know he won't leak any information about her."

"Right. Did you give him clearance this time?"

"I am getting around to it." Imko grinned and slowly typed some codes into the tablet before pausing. "How do we spell Kresso again?"

Himmy grabbed the tablet and slapped in the codes. "Idiot."

Imko wrapped his arms around his mate. "Did you call the president an idiot?"

"I called my mate an idiot. Kresso doesn't like it when he

has to fight his way in." She slapped the hand on her belly.

"I have so little fun in my daily work. Taunting my elder brother is one of my favourite things to do." He kissed her neck.

Lyra smiled at them and kept away from the wall of weapons. She looked up; the trays were empty, but she didn't feel full. She wiped her fingers on a napkin and checked her white outfit for crumbs. Maybe white wasn't the best instinct.

She sipped at the tea and waited while the couple slowly made out until there was a bit of a ruckus from outside the long doors with security locks.

Lyra stood up and looked toward the door when Imko walked up to it and opened two panels of glass with a grin. The man who came through the doors almost made Imko look delicate.

The man was huge, carrying a heavy pack and another bag draped over his torso. "Right. Where is the patient?"

Lyra was staring at him in shock, and when Imko pointed to her, she felt put on the spot. She darted to the wall, got the cylinder, and put it in front of her.

Her voice was clear. "No way is *that* getting anywhere near me."

His black hair and green eyes showed his resemblance to Imko, but the thick neck, wide shoulders, and huge hands were off the scale that had her shaking. His scent curled toward her and started that reaction between her thighs.

Oh, fuck.

CHAPTER THREE

There was an armed omega in the room, and the scent of her arousal was luring him in. It went from luring to mocking him, and he was not in the mood to be mocked. Kresso looked past his half-brother and charged into the room, dropping his equipment on the way.

The force blast to the chest threw him backward, and his brother caught him.

Himmy shouted, "Lyra, no!"

The small creature frowned and aimed at him again.

Himmy walked toward her and kept herself between the pearly woman and Kresso.

There was a frown on the woman's face. "Himmy, step aside. He's dangerous."

"He wouldn't hurt us."

"Not you. Me. He's going to hurt me."

"He's a doctor. He isn't going to hurt you. He handles me and the baby all the time. He's not dangerous. He just looks it."

The small woman glared at him around his sister-in-law. "I don't trust him."

"I won't leave you alone with him, Lyra. He won't do anything to upset you. I just need you to put the blast staff down before the guards take you down." Himmy was approaching her calmly, and she put her hand out. "Please, Lyra. Give me the staff."

Kresso straightened and watched as the tiny woman shrank a piece of tech that she had no business activating and handed it to Himmy an instant before the guards behind her threw her to the floor and pinned her hands behind her back.

They cuffed her and hauled her to her feet. Himmy was

protesting, but Imko grabbed her and said, "It's for the best that she's restrained."

Kresso's mouth dropped open when the tiny thing said, "Your first night as lovers must have been hilarious."

Himmy snorted and did it again when the woman slid her hands free of the large cuffs and massaged her wrists.

"Lyra, this is Imko's brother and the specialist he called in to be discreet." Himyana's lips were quivering in amusement. "Kresso, this is the first of the omega project results. Omega Yten Lyra."

The guards were staring at the cuffs on the ground.

"In that case, you are now my patient, Miss. I will take charge of her now, gentlemen." He wanted to growl and break their arms for touching her, but first, he wanted to gather her to him, wrap his arms around her, and bury his nose against her neck.

They pulled back, and Kresso stepped forward. The blue-haired imp that had pulled the trigger looked up at him with violet eyes. She was growling at him with an adorable tone. He grinned slowly.

Imko was dismissing the guards and locking the doors. He triggered a set of metal shutters and then nodded to Kresso. "This is the patient. We need to know what she is and what's going on in her body. She has eaten several pounds of food but is still hungry, so can we cover where the food is going first? She's concerned."

Kresso looked at the small woman who was glaring at him. "She doesn't look like she wants an exam."

Himmy came up and took the woman's hand. "She wants one. She needs to know what is going on as well. Don't you, Lyra?"

The pearl woman with blue hair calmed down at Himmy's touch. She grumped. "Yes. I do."

She was glaring at him, and he chuckled. "If you are what I think you are, your attitude is hilarious."

She growled again.

Grinning, Kresso went to get his pack. His half-brother watched over things as the med equipment emerged, and he tried to figure out what to start with.

If he had his way, she would be impaled on his cock, growling and hissing at him, but that would be inappropriate with Himmy and Imko in the room. He wondered if he could get them to leave.

Lyra felt the hackles on the back of her neck rise. Her body was hot, and the growl was vibrating out of her. The feeling of her sternum humming in her chest was distracting and definitely not human.

The hulk came back toward her and looked around. He nodded and picked her up before setting her on a round table. "This is where we will do the exam, and you won't be confined in any way unless you attack me."

She pressed her thighs together and clenched her jaw. "You should be safe."

He chuckled. "Back in a moment. Himmy, please, keep her quiet."

Lyra looked at her new acquaintance.

Himyana stood next to the table and blinked at her. "You had an . . . interesting response to Kresso."

"Yeah, that's the word for it," Lyra muttered.

"So, how do you feel about him?"

Lyra softly murmured, "I am between clawing his face and fucking him. I can feel my heartbeat everywhere. My body is making a mess."

Himmy stared at her thighs, which were thankfully masked by the dress. "Seriously?"

"Yup. This is humiliating. I just went off when I caught his scent."

Himmy looked at her. "You didn't when you scented Imko?"

"No. His scent was mixed in with yours. It made it wrong."

There was relief in the pregnant woman's eyes. "Right. He mentioned that."

Kresso returned to the table. "I suppose you also don't know that the MaKorith have excellent hearing."

Lyra frowned. "I know, but I really want to start punching and kicking you right now, and I think my body is trying to sort responses to different stimuli."

He set a series of scanning objects down and opened a small tablet terminal of sorts. "Right. We are going to go from the top down. Remain still."

She stood, and he began the scans from the head down. She breathed him in the entire time and was shaking so fast she nearly vibrated when he walked around the table before running scans on her ass and thighs.

"Well, you have excellent self-control and an extremely aggressive digestive system. The food you ate earlier has already completely turned to blood and muscle and energy."

"So, what is the waste setup like?"

Kresso blinked. "You don't know?"

"I just woke up in this body this morning. I don't know how long I was in it previously, but I know this isn't my species, and I don't know how it works. So, Kresso, tell me how I work."

He stared at her. "You don't know?"

"You keep saying that. No. I don't know. I know there was a blank, and my mind ended up inside it. I know I was dead on my world and alive here, but this is not any kind of afterlife I would have predicted, so it is another world and an alien-to-me body, and I have to learn how it works."

The huge man in front of her blinked.

"Explain it to me as you would to a child. I can ask prompting questions if you like."

"Certainly. That would help. What do you want to know?"

"So, how will I dispose of waste?"

"You have a bladder, a urethra, and a colony of kidneys for maximum filtration. So, your urine will carry out all residual materials."

"Okay. Great. I will avoid asparagus." She smiled. "Can this body get pregnant, or is it a toy?"

He blinked and checked the scans. "Four ovaries, each with a different genetic signature. A split womb for multiple carries. Theoretically, you could go into heat twice in a row with a partner and have offspring one cycle apart."

"Fine. My teeth feel weird. Tense and bitey. What is that about?"

He looked surprised. "Ah, I missed that on the first scan. You have specific teeth for mating purposes."

Her hand went to her mouth, and she felt the points along her gumline. "They are up high."

"They come down when you are aroused. May I demonstrate?"

She was wary, but she said, "Sure."

He just opened his mouth and flashed her his fangs. She leaned in and looked, reaching out to touch one fang and yelped when his tongue circled her finger and tugged it into his mouth. It was wet, hot, and surprisingly soft as he sucked on her digit. She gasped and moaned a little, and then she felt it. Her teeth came down.

She pulled her hand from his mouth with a jerk and covered her mouth with the other hand.

He chuckled and moved her hand away, lifting her lip to check on her teeth. "Very pretty. A little venom, too."

He took a quick sample, shook the vial, and put it in what seemed to be some kind of spectrum analyzer.

He reached for her skirt with another tiny vial in his free hand and slid his hand up her inner thigh to collect a fluid sample. He was spoiled for choice. He pulled his hand out from under her skirt, and it was gleaming.

The sample vial had to be wiped clean before being slotted into another analyzer.

He brought his hand toward his face and then licked at his fingers.

Lyra was stunned and just stood there, staring.

Himyana cocked her head. "Are you done, Kresso?"

"Just one more test. Audio output." He smiled. "That one can be down on the floor."

She nodded and stepped to the edge of the table before jumping down. "Audio output?" She was just pretending that the previous contacts hadn't happened and part of her core hadn't melted just because she sniffed him and he sucked her finger.

Himyana nodded and stroked her belly. "The Su'ath have a very pronounced sense of hearing, and they used to have a type of siren in their omega bloodlines. If you are Su'ath by origin, you might have those skills as well. Audio control or sub-sonic and hyper-sonic signals."

"In regular speech?"

"They sing."

"Oh, I am not good at singing."

Kresso chuckled. "This isn't a judgment of your singing voice, just your audio output. If you have the secondary vocal cords, they will be apparent on the sampling."

She nodded and scooted closer to Himmy for protection. "How do you know about the voices, Himmy?"

She grimaced. "That was how they caught us. Sonic attack. We just went down. I looked up the attacks later and found the reference to the sirens calling their mates."

"You think I am one of them?"

"I think we need to know if you are or aren't."

Kresso got more equipment together and rigged a mic that attached to Lyra's ear and was suspended in front of her lips.

"Okay. Sing anything."

Lyra blushed. "I am really bad at singing."

"It doesn't matter. Yell, scream. Whatever."

Lyra closed her eyes, opened her mouth, and sang a scale.

Kresso said softly. "Do it again."

Lyra sang scales up and down until he said, "Got it."

She exhaled and took the earpiece off. "So, what passes for music here?"

Kresso smiled. "Ask Himmy. She used to be in a band before she became a defender on Peltin."

Lyra looked at Himmy. "You did?"

"Thanks, Kresso. Folks have mostly forgotten that." Himmy sighed.

"You still have a fan club in the guards." Kresso was smiling as he went through readouts.

Himmy narrowed her eyes at him. "Zip it, brother."

Imko was standing and entering notes into a tablet. He

glanced toward the metal shutters and scowled.

Lyra caught on. "The research station wants me back in their custody."

Himmy clutched her hand and then yanked her in for a hug. Lyra squawked as she was held against the other woman, and she returned the hug.

Kresso chuckled. "One way or another, Himmy, you can't keep her."

Imko snorted. "You sure about that?"

"Brother, if I am in rut and she is on the other side of the wall, I am going through it."

Lyra rotated Himmy so that she was between her and Kresso.

Himmy started laughing. "Sorry, sweet. Imko would get me out of the way, and you would be on your own."

"Five minutes of letting her body speak to mine, and she wouldn't be hiding anymore." Kresso sounded smug.

Lyra looked around her new friend. *Yup.* He looked smug. A giant smug elf. He stared at her, and she hid behind Himmy. He laughed.

Himmy stroked her hair, and Lyra sighed. "You are going to be a good mom."

Himmy paused and said, "Thanks, Lyra."

Lyra got a hug, and the baby kicked merrily.

Kresso stood up, amusement danced in his eyes. "How long do you think you can hide behind her, Yten Lyra?"

Lyra relaxed her grip, but Himmy didn't. "Well, she's gonna keep getting bigger for a while, so I can do it for a bit."

Imko laughed. Himmy snorted. Kresso sighed.

He walked over, released Himmy's arms, and plucked Lyra out, walking to the couch and sitting with her on his lap. "I don't know if I will be the one you end up with, but I do want to savour the experience of having the first omega in decades on my lap."

Imko chuckled. "I guess you are staying for dinner. What did the test results determine?"

He settled on the couch with one arm around her waist and the other draped over her thighs. "Well, she isn't Su'ath. She's

Dimorian on the skin, Rai-Shell in the heart and lungs, her scent glands are MaKorith, her voice is Su'ath, and her reproductive and digestive systems are unknown, but I would guess they were Hallovien. The hair and eyes are unknown. The body style is based on MaKorith omegas."

Lyra blinked. "Scent glands?"

Kresso wrapped his hand around her neck and rubbed the side of her throat with his thumb. "Right here. Yours are still developing."

"There are more?"

He chuckled. "Between your thighs, under your arms. Just in case your alpha is completely blind. Well, your alphas. You are set for more than one, which was probably part of the design."

She looked into his sparkling green eyes and swallowed. "So, why am I on your lap?"

"So that when Imko dangles you in front of the generals, I will have a memory of holding our first omega in decades."

Imko snorted. "I am going to let her pick the first hundred by scent. Only men without mates will be asked to apply, and they all have to be sufficiently talented enough to defend her when others try to take her."

Lyra felt his hands tighten on her and squeaked. Kresso relaxed his grip and exhaled.

Lyra was fighting a lot of instinct. She wanted to lean against his shoulder and breath him in. There was an urge to squirm against him and another to touch his face and calm him. Touching him anywhere else would *not* calm him.

"So, why exactly do I react so violently to . . . um . . . you?" She looked at Kresso. "And what is with the copious lubrication?"

He grinned. "You have two glands inside your sex that provide you with the necessary lubrication. Alphas are larger than betas, and the knot around the base of our cocks can be difficult to manage without sufficient slick."

She stared at him and knew her eyes were wide. Her voice was a squeak. "What?"

Himmy sighed. "I think we need to have the sex talk, Lyra."

Imko grinned. "I want to listen in."

Himyana swatted him on the arm. "No. Bad president!"

Himyana grabbed Lyra's hand and yanked her out of Kresso's lap. With surprising speed, she bustled Lyra into the bathroom and explained how things worked with betas and alphas and how much lube was necessary in the beginning, and then she explained, "Omegas are built for sex with alphas. You naturally secrete the necessary lubrication, your inner tissues stretch to accept the most awkwardly large of alphas, and your ass also lubes itself when there is a second male and you are in heat."

Lyra put her hand on her ass. "But it isn't connected to any—oh."

"Yeah. I looked through the old archives and memoirs of the lost omegas. Imko made me stop. I kept feeding him sexy thoughts through our link and distracting him while he was trying to do political stuff. Omegas are basically walking hormones who keep alphas calm so they can be productive. By taking out their lust on you, they can spend more time with their brains functioning in a more useful manner than focusing on finding something they can fuck."

Lyra frowned. "What?"

"Omegas are horny and cuddly; alphas are horny and hyper-intelligent. With the horny out of the way, the hyper-intelligent can shine."

Lyra cocked her head. "How do you and Imko . . ." She rotated her hand.

"At first, lots of lube and stretching with his fingers. After a few months, he would purr in my ear, and my body would start getting ready. Now, he just has to say my name a certain way, and things start happening. Add that to pregnancy hormones, and I spend most of my day avoiding him or trying to get him inside me. The bump is making it a challenge, but Imko is creative."

Lyra chuckled. "So, why don't the alphas just all have betas?"

"They don't have the patience or self-control for it. Also, the ones who do have betas tend to have more than one. A beta can only have one baby for an alpha, so for a second child, they need a second beta. That is how Imko came into the world. His father and his mother are retired now and living a relaxing life in the southern reaches."

"What about Kresso's mother?"

"She died birthing him. That happens a lot as well. It's another reason that the alphas avoid betas as breeding partners. They don't want to see their partner die."

Lyra blinked. "Oh. So, how do you send Imko signals?"

"Right. Now, after you have found a lover and want to connect permanently, the alpha bites you." As she spoke, she pulled the neckline of her dress aside and showed the mark on the left side of her neck. "The bite provides the link that helps keep the child alive, and it dampens any pheromones I would normally give off when I am receptive so another alpha can't consider me available." She straightened her collar. "I have bitten him, too, but all it does is let him know when he's going at it too hard."

Lyra blushed. "Um, right. Why did they mention multiple partners? It is a strange concept to me, and I want to make sure I am understanding it."

"Ah, since omegas are pacifiers by nature, they tend to take more than a single mate. A unit forms around them and is a solid fighting component. They defend their omega, so they are assigned to the outer colonies to act as protectors. If she or he is in danger, they are fierce and deadly, so the omega is the catalyst to defending the colony."

"Wait. There are male omegas?"

"Not anymore. They died with the females."

"How did the destruction spread so far?"

She sighed. "The researchers that were trying to destroy the omegas inoculated the teams first. The alphas infected their own omegas with the destructive variant that killed them. That caused a lot of suicides and left the outer colonies without anchor teams."

Lyra crossed her arms and leaned against the sink. "Well, that explains something."

"What?"

"Why they made me from so many species. A series of species would have to be involved in taking out the omegas again. This patchwork system makes for a more resistant immune response."

"Oh. That makes sense, but who did it?"

Lyra grimaced. "Did any Su'ath have MaKorith omegas?"

"Uh, yeah. They captured a few."

"Before or after the inoculation?"

"Afte—oh. Their omegas died, too."

"How much information do you share with the other species? It is entirely likely that this situation eventually became airborne and took out omegas across this whole region. Someone put the bodies together, and I am part of the third wave. The other two weren't viable, so someone has been mixing and matching with cloned ingredients."

"You can't know that for certain."

Lyra tapped her temple. "They pulled a dying consciousness from another world. That is about as cobbled together as you can get."

"Oh. Right. And your kind doesn't have omegas."

"Nope. My body knows what it wants to do, but my brain is a little appalled." She snorted. "Very appalled."

"But . . . you do feel attraction for Kresso, right? He's a strong male, unattached, and very intelligent."

"Yeah. Attraction isn't the word. I want to jump onto his body and hold on until he fucks me. For me, that is not a normal impulse." She grimaced. "And I am supposed to help pick out of a hundred or so? What if one is enough or two?"

"Then they will bribe you into taking on a third or possibly a fifth. Our family gatherings will become large in a hurry."

"If I end up with Kresso as my first. If not, I will be someone else's family."

Himyana blinked. "I hadn't thought of that. I mean, you shot him with a stun bolt. That has to be some kind of foreplay."

They giggled and left the restroom. Imko looked up from his tablet. "The scent samples will be here in two days. Clips of you have already been sent out."

"Clips?"

Himmy smiled. "Images generated from the security cameras here and the files at the research facility. They made a three-dimensional model with your original exam specifications."

"Wait, so there are holograms zipping around as bait to try and get folks to sign up for the run?"

Imko snorted. "Of course not. The images are just to taunt folks into sending in scent packs."

"What's a scent pack?" She frowned.

Kresso smirked, went to the tea trays, got a napkin and wiped it along his neck, hands, armpits and groin. He tossed it to her. "That is a scent pack."

She caught the napkin. The scent of male, musk, sex, and heat caught her off guard. She thudded to the ground when her knees gave way. "Oh."

She used her fingertips to fold the napkin and put it on the floor. "That's embarrassing."

Kresso crouched in front of her. "That is rather heartening." He was grinning knowingly.

"Stop smirking."

"Why? This is the most fun I have had in years. Would you like some help to your feet?"

She gritted her teeth. "No. I will be fine. Shoo!" She flapped her hand at him.

Himmy started to laugh, and Imko had to hold her up. Her face was red, and she was wheezing with her violent amusement.

Imko was laughing as well.

Kresso moved behind Lyra, lifted her to her feet, and settled in a chair with her on his lap. "That was a very telling response."

She grumped. "Ya think?"

"So, I suppose I should go and work on my speed and accuracy."

"Well, it did take you an entire hour to get here. You are going to end up being at the bottom of the pile if you don't speed things up."

He stroked her cheek and smiled. "I will speed things up."

"Um, okay."

She was going to make a move to leave, but he kissed her, and her wits shattered.

She heard Imko bark an order, but Kresso kept slowly kissing her, his lips gliding against hers. Her body was taking its cues from him, and she leaned up and gripped his head, pulling him closer.

Imko's voice got sharp, and hands pulled her away from Kresso. She whimpered and sobbed while Himmy pulled her away. Imko looked at her in astonishment, and Kresso looked at her grimly and got up. "I will be back when she is choosing."

He collected his equipment, looked at her one more time, and left the way he had come. Imko lifted the shutters a moment before Kresso looked like he would have punched his way through it.

Lyra gradually became aware that she was whining and crying, and Himmy was trying to calm her. *What the actual fuck just happened?*

CHAPTER FOUR

Lyra sat with Himmy, and she couldn't stop pouting. Ever since Kresso had left, she had been moping and having tantrums like a toddler. She never pouted, and tantrums were new. Himmy laughed and said she was good practice.

The samples were in, and there were three hundred eighty-five. Himmy was there to help her through the sniff test, but the electrodes on her head and neck would accurately determine how she responded to the different scents.

The researchers were eager to see how she responded, and she sat at the table so the cameras could get a look at her while the first batch of samples was brought to her.

She opened the first one and wrinkled her nose. "This one has a mate."

She had four unremarkable samples, and then she laughed. "This is the mate to the first sample."

She continued on for fifty more samples before she found one that set her off. "Uh, save this one for the keep pile?"

Himmy exhaled in relief.

They kept going, and she found Kresso's sample with a grin and set him on the keep pile.

In the end, she had thirty selections that sped up her heartbeat.

The researchers were grinning and congratulating themselves.

Lyra was shaking, and Himmy put an arm around her and walked her out.

"Do you need to spend some time alone?" Himmy asked quietly.

"Uh. Yeah. I think so. That was . . . a lot."

"Poor baby. Come on. Let's get you to your collection."

Lyra snorted.

Kresso had begun courting her . . . from a distance. She had gotten flowers and clothing and her all-time favourite, a dildo that was supposedly equivalent to Kresso. It helped to take the edge off, and she had gotten most of it inside her, but she was pretty sure that the knot was a two-person event.

Himmy smiled. "Call me when you are ready to have tea."

"Give me an hour."

Lyra stumbled into her room, stripped, and grabbed the toy before climbing into bed and making herself scream.

The sex drive had caught her by surprise once it was set off. It didn't stop. There were moments of a slow simmer, but her body was always ready to climb onto her alpha. Now that she had caught the scents of the other suitables, Kresso was still her favourite, but there were some close seconds. Very close.

After she had showered and changed with the morning's slick-covered dress in the cleaner, she was sitting and having tea with Himmy.

"So, how do you feel about this morning's events?"

Lyra shrugged. "I came four times, so the last hour was eventful."

Himmy snorted. "That wasn't what I meant, but good for you. I do envy the omega constitution."

Lyra snickered. "That sounds like a rule of sexual quotas for omegas."

Himmy chuckled. "I will mention the quota idea to Kresso. I am pretty confident that he is going to make it into your alpha collection."

"Pretty confident?"

"Oh, yeah." She sipped her tea. "He has been doing speed runs and working out."

"How much effect could that have in a few days?"

Himmy laughed a bright and happy sound. "Oh, this is going to be fun."

On the day of the Omega Run, Lyra stood in a snug bodysuit similar to that of the flyers, and she had sleeves loaded with projectiles that would continue to advance as she fired them into the course.

She wasn't allowed to see the alphas who were going to chase after her scent, but she had the location of the capsule that would protect her while they chased after her. Her goal was to get to that capsule.

She swallowed and looked at the gate that would open into the woods. She had walked them the night before and woven a few false trails. If they followed an old scent, they were suckers.

She watched the clock, and when it reached zero, the doors opened, and she ran.

Trees and branches clogged the paths, so she fired lures into the outer reaches and under trees in pulled roots. Lyra felt the branches lashing at her face and pulling at her hair, but this was the most like herself that she had felt since waking up at the research station.

She was through half of the drops and had fifty to go. This was the most fun she had had with two feet on the ground. The hair-trigger orgasm was enjoyable as well.

Lyra climbed a rope ladder into the trees and continued the second portion of the route. She stopped and sent the disks into the canopy of the trees until she had completely expended her markers, and then she got to the final spot and stepped into the capsule. It sealed around her, and she waited. In the distance, she heard a roar that was oddly familiar for a sound she hadn't heard before. Her stomach flipped, and her sex throbbed.

They were coming, and she was on the edge.

Himyana looked at her husband. "I swear, if they hurt her . . ."

Imko blinked. "They all got a little . . . savage. I haven't seen Kresso that bulked out since his first rut."

"The others were all fairly alpha'd out as well. I haven't seen that kind of a collection of aggression . . . ever." She looked at him and chuckled. "Well, our wedding night."

"But there was only one of me. That is why we use the secure pod. They won't be able to get to her. Hopefully. This hasn't been done in generations."

They watched the flashes of light on the screen that indicated the alphas who were pursuing Lyra's scent.

Himmy pointed at one dot that blurred back and forth with amazing speed. "Who's that?"

Imko chuckled. "Who do you think? You are going to have a sister-in-law."

Himmy grinned and felt both relief and nervousness for Lyra. Kresso had bulked out alarmingly, and his eyes had been glittering as Lyra's scent was presented to the males waiting to go. He had always been big, but now, he looked dangerous. He had always been a slightly grumpy giant to her, and now that his mind was on mating her new friend, he looked like a monster. It was a good thing that Lyra seemed to be hot for him as well. Hopefully, they wouldn't hurt each other . . . much.

Lyra could see the trees thrashing around, and then there was a thud near her, and someone wrenched her pod out of the tree, and they took flight back toward the base.

She squeaked and braced herself on the inside of the tube as the blur of the forest went past until they were back at the starting line. She was carried over the line and saw a dark gold hand dump a bag full of markers into a counter. Fifty-one.

Her pod was set on the platform, and she was pretty sure it was Kresso that had carried her in, but he wasn't letting her see him.

An alpha in a deep blue bodysuit charged out of the woods, and he dumped his catch bag into the counter. Forty-nine.

Lyra swallowed as he looked into the pod, put his forehead against it, and purred. His eyes were as dark as his suit, and his hair was a rich red-brown. His expression was needy, and his body was terrifying. She wanted to touch him.

His mating fangs were down and thick. The venom that would tie them together gleamed on the tips. She whined and pressed against the inside of the tube.

His fingers clenched on the outside of the tube, and she heard claws scrape. She had no idea they had claws. Himmy never mentioned claws.

There was a growl from behind her, and a huge body thudded into the one on the tube, and they were fighting.

She saw teeth and claws. Kresso had gotten a bulked-out makeover, and he still looked really hot to her hormone-glazed eyes.

The men emerging from the woods looked at her and then at the two men fighting on the ground. Three of them got together, sidled around the edge of the fight, and headed toward her pod.

She felt her self-defence emergency measure between her shoulders, and she waited while the three rushed her pod to grab it, and she lifted her head and screamed. A second later, they dropped her as her two mates tackled them and beat the shit out of them.

The pod was on its side, and she watched the blood fly on either side of her. When silence fell, a blood-stained Kresso came to her and lifted the pod to a standing position.

"There you go, sweet. The man behind you is Mahel."

She twisted, and the alpha with the dark-blue eyes smiled at her. "Hello, dearling. Aren't you cute?"

Lyra sighed. *Cute* for an alpha was related to hot and sexy for anyone else.

She worried her lip a little, and her little fangs were down.

"What does a slip of a girl need fangs for?"

Kresso chuckled. "If she bites us, we are only going to create omegas for the rest of our lives. No alphas, no sons. No betas, just endless little daughters."

Mahel grinned. "I like the idea of a lot of little omegas with her hair and my eyes."

Lyra blinked. "Oh. *That* is what my venom is for."

Kresso chuckled. "Indeed. The only thing it could be for was to affect your alphas, so I ran some tests on semen, and it does some interesting things."

Mahel was purring again as he pressed close to her. "What

kind of interesting things?"

"I believe they will be enhanced omegas, but we need to get her to gestation to prove it," Kresso growled in a deep and sexy way. "I do love a long-term experiment."

She looked at the huge bodies pressing against the pod and was a little bit grateful for the barrier . . . for now. She was gonna get smooshed. Over half of her body was all for it.

The alphas who didn't fight grinned and filed off through an open door. Medics came out and tended to the three that tried to snag her.

Imko came toward them and nodded. "Well, Lyra. It seems you have your first mates. Kresso ni Lyra and Mahel ni Lyra, we have your transport to a more private space where you can complete the process."

"*Complete the process.* Yeah, that sounds hot," Lyra muttered.

Mahel chuckled.

"Wait. You know who this guy is?" Lyra jerked her thumb at Mahel.

Imko snorted. "Yeah. I know him. Kresso knows him. Ninety percent of the population knows him."

She looked at him, and he was grinning at her. "Can I get an STD test on him before we go any further? A guy known by that many people has to have picked something up."

He looked hurt. "We were all cleared before we were allowed to send a scent sample."

She exhaled. "Oh. Okay."

Kresso murmured, "And our scents would have told you if we were infected."

She nodded and looked at Mahel. "Sorry if I offended you. I don't have a very good opinion of popular people in general."

He nodded. "He just said they knew who I was; he never said I was popular."

"Oh. Good point." She pressed her hand to the inside of the pod. He placed his hand over hers, and she swallowed. "Oh boy."

Kresso chuckled. "We will take it easy on you."

Mahel muttered, "Speak for yourself."

Imko grinned. "Lyra, Himmy wants you here when she goes into labour. I expect your mates to make sure that you are there."

Lyra smiled. "I think that ten days will be enough to take the edge off."

Her mates looked at her with amusement.

Imko shook his head with a grin. "You come back for the birth, and then you can return for another ten days."

"Wait. How long is normal?"

Imko chuckled. "I hid Himyana away for forty days before they came looking for us."

Kresso snorted. "You mean before we found you."

He shrugged. "Himmy was used to me by the time you found us."

Lyra grinned. "She told me she was desperate for food cooked by anyone else. You have an issue with seasoning, Imko. You need to use some."

Imko smiled. "You are not going to be so amused when they finish with you."

She decided to play and let big tears fill her eyes. "They won't want me anymore?"

Imko blinked. "Uh . . ."

Kresso growled at his younger brother. "You upset her."

Mahel was snarling and holding the capsule close.

She sighed and cleared her features. "Don't worry about it, Imko. I am sure you will be all smug with the next omega that wakes up. Threatening virgins with alpha cocks isn't polite."

He flushed and winced. "You are going to tell Himmy about that, aren't you?"

"Oh, yes. Doesn't matter that I have ridden Kresso's toy so much that I have worn it out. It's still mean."

Kresso's eyes got hot. "Where is the transport?"

Imko chuckled. "Other side of the trees. It's coming down now."

Lyra saw the ship descending, and Mahel lifted her capsule and started walking off with her. She heard Imko saying they were registered to her now, so he wished Kresso the best of luck.

Kresso was with them before they left the trees, and the pod was set in a slot and strapped down. She knew she wasn't getting out of the pod until they got where they were going, which was why her pod had life support. It also contained her sweaty scent, so it didn't add fuel to their fire.

Lyra tried to get comfortable at the bottom of the pod. "So, how long is our flight?"

Kresso growled. "Half an hour. I could get us there faster."

Mahel snorted. "So could I, but I am saving my energy for better pursuits."

She looked at him and asked, "Tell me about yourself. What do you do, what are your hobbies, what type of woman do you prefer?"

She saw Kresso shaking his head at Mahel. "Kresso, I already know about you. Himmy told me all about the women that gathered at the med centre in hopes of a personal exam. I am guessing that Mahel has something similar going on."

Mahel spoke quietly, "I run a base in one of the colonies. I am in charge of the personnel. I play the Ythal harp, and as for women, I pay for whatever is available at the brothel."

Kresso put his hand over his face and groaned.

"Oh. Can you still get it up if you don't have to pay for it?" Lyra asked him directly.

Mahel blinked. "Pretty sure that it won't be a problem."

Kresso scowled. "What the hell? You read me the riot act."

Lyra snorted. "It was only over the com. If you flirt with them, it is like feeding wild beasts. They want to come and sit in your hand . . . so to speak. Brothels are transactional. I read up on them. The women who get into it do it for short-term financial gain. Same with the men. Fucking for cash is less intimate than flirting."

She shrugged. "Don't get me wrong, and if I smell another woman on any part of you, it will be the last time you touch me for a very long time. Either one of you."

Kresso smiled. "No objections, but I always heard that omegas were generous when it came to sex."

"They may have been. I am part of a new batch. Until I am sure of both of you, I reserve the right to be jealous and paranoid."

Mahel sighed. "I could just curl up with my nose against your skin and breathe you in for a few hours. In fact, I might eventually be sated enough to do that. Eventually."

She snorted and waited.

Kresso smiled. "You wore the toy out?"

She chuckled. "An exaggeration. I also never took the knot with it. I thought I should wait for the cock to have a flesh and blood alpha attached."

Mahel paused. "You gave her a toy?"

"A life model of my cock. She was curious." He grinned and patted the pod.

"So, um, guys. Your current appearance is a hormonal thing?"

Mahel chuckled. "Isn't it interesting? A little sniff of omega perfume, and I am ready to punch through a piece of steel to get to you. Not necessarily with my fists."

Lyra sat there with her eyes wide.

Kresso explained, "We are faster, stronger, and our senses are keener. But we are also rock hard and want to be inside you, which is why you are staying in the pod until we land and get you to the retreat."

"Retreat?"

"Yes, we are going to one of the presidential islands. There are food and clothing stores set up. It is uninhabited, and there is one building on the entire landmass."

The ship started descending, and the guys stood up, unstrapping her pod from the groove in the floor. Mahel carried her off the transport, and when Kresso was off, it flew away.

Kresso led the way off the beach and down a well-tended path that expanded into a huge house surrounded by a covered porch. Mahel carried her inside and set the pod down in a bedroom that had a rack of her dresses in it. The size meant they weren't for anyone else.

Mahel bent low. "If you want to keep your action suit, change into something we can get under or shred. The release to the pod is under your left foot."

She nodded. "Got it. Now shoo."

Kresso laughed. "That is her way of saying we should leave her for a moment."

They left the room, and she crunched her heel down on the left side of the pod. There was a click, a whir, and then the top split open. She put her hands on the open lip and levered herself out of the pod before dropping to the side.

She unsealed her suit and picked one of the white dresses that felt like it was made of soft cotton, and when the suit came off, the dress went on. She pulled her hair up and let it drop straight down her back. She brushed her hands down her skirt and opened the door. To her relief and confusion, they were not waiting for her. She lifted her head and sniffed and found them easily. The amount of musk they were putting out was dizzying.

She walked on bare feet through the building and found them in the kitchen making up trays with beverages, fruit, and other readily edible items.

"Whatcha doin'?" She walked toward them and continued to get high off their scents. Her body was reacting, and this was the place and time for it.

Kresso chuckled. "We are laying in food and beverages so that we can stay ensconced with you and keep your energy levels up. First nights can be taxing."

She glanced outside. "Nights?"

Mahel put a tray on his forearm and another on the palm of his hand. A third went on his other palm. "You open doors, pet."

She nodded. "Fine, but I don't know where we are going."

Kresso picked up two trays and grinned. "Follow me."

He led the way into the cool halls of the house, and the set of double doors was where he stopped. She slipped forward and did her job. She opened the doors and got out of the way while they brought in the supplies. The table they set them on was soon full, and Mahel got a small disk from a drawer and set it in the centre of the assembled trays. "That will keep the area a few degrees cooler than the surrounding air."

"Oh, goody." She smiled.

Kresso stripped off his suit and settled against the massive white wood headboard. She swallowed the sudden rush of saliva, and when he beckoned to her, she jolted forward, and a soft whine came from her throat. He was shiny gold, and his muscles gleamed invitingly.

"Come here, Lyra. I want to take in your scent and rub you all over me."

She looked over her shoulder. "What about Mahel?"

"He has to wait," Kresso growled.

She scowled as the growl made her uneasy, and she stepped away from him.

He grinned, and she found herself in his lap.

"How did you . . . I didn't see you move." She felt a hot throbbing against her thigh.

"I promise that I will move slowly from here on in." He chuckled.

"So, isn't this . . . uh . . . mean to Mahel?"

Kresso chuckled. "He should have been faster. I could have taken seventy-five of your targets and destroyed the rest, but I took pity on him and let him beat up the others for their tokens."

Mahel murmured, "Kresso being ahead of me kept me moving fast. His speed was legendary, and it seems he has resurrected it for you."

"But I will use it for you and not with you." Kresso chuckled. "Now, mate, I would like a kiss from you."

She looked at him with his glittering green eyes focused on her. "Are you coming down, or do I stand up? Your junk may be in danger if I do."

He smiled and threaded his hand in her hair. "I will always come to you if you need me to."

Lyra was trying to think of a witty response to that when his lips touched hers. Her breath caught, and her blood surged in her veins. His lips moved over hers, and she sighed softly, leaning into him.

She licked at his lips, and his tongue teased hers. She pressed her hand to his chest and the other to his cheek. His skin was hot, and his muscles were tense. He had a lot of them, and they weren't in a standard configuration. She wanted to look and stare and lick, but instead, she concentrated on not tensing up when his hand dragged her skirt up with his fingers on the inside of her right leg.

Lyra froze when his fingers found the slick between her thighs, and he moved his hand against her clit. The whine that came from her throat was hoarse, needy, and desperate.

He brushed his lips against hers. "That sounded fun."

The shiver was a full-body experience. She whispered, "How is this going to work?"

"That is up to you, but I think getting you out of this dress is key to things moving on. Having seen your scans, I am actually eager to see all of you."

She blushed. "I will get up and take it off."

He chuckled and removed his fingers from between her thighs before slowly licking them. She saw claws.

"Where did the claws come from? You didn't have them the day I met you."

Mahel growled, "You two have met?"

She turned her head and looked at her other mate. "He was the physician who ran the scans on me when I first woke up. He explained my physiology to me. Not sex. Himmy explained that."

Mahel was sitting in a chair near the door, and he was looking at her with focus. "She explained sex to you?"

"Yeah. I wasn't born to a species with knotting in their mating practices. So, she gave me the answers to the questions, and now I think I know what is happening next." She frowned. "I still feel bad that Mahel isn't with us."

Kresso chuckled. "If it makes you feel better, he can join us. I just didn't want you overwhelmed."

She looked at him and pulled his head down to hers. "I am going to be overwhelmed no matter who I am with. Besides, with two of you, I won't catch a draft."

Mahel laughed and got to his feet. He started to strip. "I am taking that as an invitation."

Kresso chuckled. "There is no getting him back into that suit now."

The sound of shredding fabric sent a ripple of adrenalin

through her, and her dress was rendered ineffective as cover in a matter of seconds. Mahel joined them, and his claws shredded the rest of the dress before he pressed against her back and buried his face against her neck. Kresso did the same, and as they breathed her in, she let go of her self-control and let the lust roll over her. For the first time in her life, she let her body take the lead.

CHAPTER FIVE

They breathed her in for what felt like hours and purred while they did it.

"Himmy didn't mention the purring would feel like this." Lyra squirmed, and they adjusted their position so that she was wedged between them.

Kresso chuckled. "Some betas don't like it, so their mates refrain from purring."

Mahel's hands were moving on her belly and between her thighs. He guided her thigh up onto Kresso's hip, and the pads of his fingers rubbed slow circles around her sex. "So slick and smooth. You are very hot, Lyra."

The erections against her belly and back left her whining as Kresso moved to kiss his way down her body. Mahel pulled her head back, and he licked and gnawed at her neck before turning her head for a kiss.

He growled as he kissed her, and she gasped because Kresso was between her thighs and his tongue was sliding into her with alarming depth. She was moaning into Mahel, twisting against Kresso, and when she came, they both laughed softly.

She was panting, and a fine sheen of sweat covered her skin.

Mahel slicked two fingers at her opening and moved them against her rear entrance. The claws were thankfully gone or, at least, not in evidence as he pushed a finger into her back passage. She mewled in distress and twisted against him.

He softly murmured in her ear, and when his finger was in all the way, she panted while clinging to Kresso. Mahel moved his finger slowly, and she felt the rush of fluid around his digit.

"Oh, there's the welcome I had hoped for. I have heard

about the omegas of old, and you do not disappoint." He worked a second finger into her, and she grunted as he began to thrust in and out while she whimpered as tension built in her again.

The nerves that Mahel was working were different from the ones that Kresso was teasing. His claws had also thankfully disappeared, and when he slid two fingers into her, she grunted. She twisted against both of them, and Kresso chuckled. She met his green gaze with her shocked eyes, and his thumb circled her clit, and the feeling of being stretched and invaded sent her into another orgasm which seemed to be her body's default. Every touch turned into pleasure even if her brain wasn't sure when it started.

Lyra tried to keep her human sensibilities from stopping what was going on, but she clutched at Kresso and whimpered when he slid into her with her thigh draped over his.

The feeling of being stretched was intense, and he kept his gaze locked on hers as he moved further inside her. She gasped and dug her nails into his arms. Mahel kept his fingers inside her and nipped at her neck. "Just let him in."

She was panting. "I am trying, but the angle is funny."

Mahel chuckled. "Ah. I can see I am not helpful."

Kresso flicked his gaze to Mahel, and the fingers pulled out of her ass with an embarrassing squelching sound.

She whimpered as he moved away, and she felt coolness.

Kresso whispered, "How do you want me?"

"Me up on my hands and knees, and you behind me."

He shuddered and withdrew. "You know you won't have any control over what I am doing."

She nodded. "Since I don't know what to expect, I don't have any control anyway."

He slid out of her, flipped her over, and pulled her onto her hands and knees. She had just settled when he widened her knees and his cock slid inside her again. Mahel was reclining on one arm and watching her face as Kresso worked inside her. The slick she was producing made the entry nearly frictionless, but her muscles were clenching around him and slowing him down. He moved into her when the spasms relaxed.

Kresso gripped her hips. "Almost there, Lyra."

She felt the edge of his knot pressing against her, and she tensed. His hand smoothed her waist and back. "Easy, pet."

She heard the soft sounds that were coming from her throat, and she closed her eyes. Her lids flew open when she felt lips tugging at her nipple.

Mahel was under her and used his lips, tongue, and teeth on one breast then the next. Kresso started moving inside her, and her thoughts blanked out as she surrendered to *feeling*.

Fire surrounded her, and the burn was amazing. Mahel moved around under her, caressed her clit to send her into throbbing climax after throbbing climax, and then shifted around to kiss her while she moaned and sobbed. She couldn't remain still.

Kresso's knot was getting larger, and when he couldn't push it in and withdraw it again, he shoved deep and growled. Heat flooded her belly. His knot swelled and filled her to the edge of pain. She froze and gasped, shivering with arousal in her blood and a cessation to the caresses that had built the tension.

She felt a caress on her cheek, and Mahel whispered in her ear, "Relax, Lyra. You are holding him so tight. His eyes are turning blue."

She looked at him and blinked. He was sweating, but his eyes were sparkling. She took a deep breath and tried to relax. He sank in a little further, and she tensed again. Kresso smoothed a hand down her back. "Easy, Lyra."

Mahel stroked her cheek and then did the most extraordinary thing. He leaned in, and she thought he would whisper in her ear, but he licked the tip of her pointed ear, and she collapsed to her elbows. She looked up at him, stunned. "What the hell was that?"

He grinned. "I am glad that it worked. Now relax and let your nerves do their work."

She made a questioning sound, but he licked at the tip of her ear, sucked, and it was sending the signal to her clit that a warm set of lips wrapped around it. She was confused, but her body was delighted, and she came around Kresso's cock.

He grunted, and his hands gripped her hips.

She tried to move her head away from Mahel and mewled when his hands kept her pinned. Delicate flicks of his tongue on the tip of her ear told her he knew exactly how sensitive it was.

It was another five minutes of soft licking and two more fluttering orgasms. Kresso slid free of her, and she collapsed forward onto Mahel.

He caught her with a chuckle. "Aw, sweet. You did really well for a first time. How many times did you climax?"

She rubbed her head against his chest. "Nine. Twelve. Don't know."

Kresso trailed his lips over the back of her neck. "You did really well."

She sighed. "Once I feel like I can touch you as well, things are going to go a little faster."

Mahel stilled. "You don't think you can touch us?"

"All the omega records have alphas making all the moves. There is no record of an omega being anything but frisky and compliant." She looked at his face. "According to the records, all I have to do is say yes. Well, that and make sure that you know when my heat is going to kick in, and I have no idea about that."

Mahel sighed and put her hands on his chest. "You can touch me anytime and anywhere you want to. It might get embarrassing in public, but it is a chance I am willing to take."

Kresso murmured while kissing her back, "Not while I am with a patient, but any other time, you can have your way with me."

She chuckled. "Well, in that case . . ."

She pressed Mahel to his back and climbed over him, pumping his cock a few times with her hand before she settled the flared head against her slippery sex and guided him into her.

Mahel stared at her in surprise as she settled on him with her hands braced on his abdomen, counting the different muscle clusters bulging and twitching under her touch.

She slowly started to rise and then sink on him. This time, she could focus on what she was feeling, and when he reached up to cup her breasts, she picked up the pace, and the heat stroking inside her had her closing her eyes.

Kresso kissed her as she rose and fell. She moved faster and faster when Mahel stroked her clit with small circles. She shuddered and paused while her body flexed and fluttered around him. When she opened her eyes, Mahel was grinning at her, and Kresso was chuckling. She felt half of Mahel's knot inside, and she blushed.

She eased up, and there was a popping sensation as she slipped off the knot.

Mahel chuckled. "Tired of teasing me?"

"No, but I think I will enjoy it more if you take over. I keep having to stop for . . . reasons."

Kresso moved aside, Mahel lifted her off him, and she was back on her hands and knees with him driving into her a moment later. She moaned low as he thudded into her, and very wet sounds rang in the air.

Her forehead pressed to the bedding, the scents of sex surrounded her, and the sounds rang in her ears. A hand wove in her hair and lifted her head, bending her toward him, and Mahel rested on one arm while holding and twisting her to kiss him. His tongue twined with hers and wrapped around it.

The tension on her body fought the jolting of his cock, and she whined softly, sucking at his tongue and shivering as a wave of fluttering release ran through her. He growled softly and shoved into her, spilling in heated spurts and his knot locking tight.

She panted, and he pulled her tight to his torso. She reached up and gripped his arm. He nuzzled the side of her head and said, "Hang on."

She hung on, and he used his long tongue to tease and flick her ear until she shivered around him. He eased a little deeper, and she groaned. She held onto him with her head turned toward him until he eased out slowly as his knot eased.

There was a rush of hot fluids that ran down her inner thighs, and she blushed.

Kresso took her from Mahel and hugged her. "Well done, Lyra."

She looked up at him and blinked. "Well done? What? You guys did me."

He snorted. "We all made it through the first round of coupling without anyone drawing blood or causing an injury."

"Oh. Good. I think I want to get some water."

"Well, you do lose a lot of fluid. I hadn't properly appreciated the amount of slick that you can produce." He kissed her temple.

Mahel moved behind her, and she heard him at the tray. He came back, and something hard and cold pressed to her naked shoulder.

Lyra gasped and turned to him, only to have a berry pushed between her teeth. It exploded in her mouth, was tart and sweet, and reminded her of something.

She looked at Mahel, and he grinned. She chewed and swallowed. He held the water bottle to her lips, and she swallowed greedily, gripping his wrist. When she backed away, he lowered the bottle and leaned in to kiss her.

His mouth took possession of hers, and she took in his heat and the vivid strokes of his tongue that sent sparks through her. She moaned and gripped his shoulder as the kiss went on and on. Her sharp little fangs were down, his wide blades of fangs were down, and they were both careful not to bite the other.

The kiss's frenzy finally slowed, and her breathing relaxed. He pressed his forehead to hers and chuckled. "Your scent is coming in."

Kresso laughed softly. "She's getting to full scent quickly. That took the edge off. Lyra, would you like to see our temporary home while we get used to each other?"

"Can I wash up a little? I don't want to stick to myself."

Kresso got to his feet and carried her into the bathing chamber. She was cleaned up, they were cleaned up, and a trickle of liquid slowly snaked down her inner thigh. She grumped and wiped off the traces with her fingers before going to wash her hands.

Kresso chuckled. "Don't like leaking?"

"It is disconcerting. Odd. When my proper sense of smell kicks on, I am sure it will be enthralling, but for now, it is just a tickle that's sticky."

Mahel blinked. "Your sense of smell . . ."

Kresso snorted. "Don't worry. She's fully mature. She's only been walking around for six days, so her senses are coming online one at a time. Her slick glands were the first to wake. Then her teeth."

"Wait. Is the scent thing something that comes with age?" She frowned. "I didn't get that far into my education. I haven't finished reading about puberty, and no one mentioned the ears."

Mahel laughed. "They are the last things to develop, so it was a bit of a test."

She snorted. "So glad you were sure before you participated in today's events."

Kresso grinned. "Not everyone was privy to your exact scans. Himyana, Imko, and I were the only ones who knew about your teeth and what they contain."

She touched the spots where her teeth had receded. "Is it a problem?"

Kresso shrugged. "I am fine with it."

"I can just not bite you until there's a boy."

Mahel chuckled. "I don't think we want that. I would love the chance to have a daughter."

"Wait. You said that before."

"I mean it."

Kresso chuckled. "My family can get its son out of Imko. Himmy looks to be carrying a strong little boy."

"So, we are waiting for my sense of smell to kick in?"

Mahel smiled. "Just for the marking. Your scent is coming in, so it won't be long."

"How . . . what do I smell like?"

"Hral berries."

She blushed. "Like the one you gave me."

He nodded. "Yes. They are particularly sweet when warm."

Kresso offered his hand. "Come on, Yten Lyra. We are going

to go exploring."

"Shouldn't I put something on?" She looked down at her pearl and rose body.

Mahel spoke from behind her. "Why? There is no one here. Literally. The island is secure and has no occupants. This is the only building on the entire island."

"So, there are no drones hovering around as soon as I go outside?" She perked up.

Kresso laughed. "No vids."

She walked with them out onto the huge, covered deck, and the breezes made her hair flicker and flutter. She looked at the hair tie that wrapped from the base of their skull for about six inches, keeping it all tidy. The rest of their hair flowed out of the wrap below their shoulders. She had yet to see a MaKorith male with his hair loose.

She was hesitant but slowly walked out into the light, spied a path, and headed into the woods with the soft sand under her feet. The path led to a meadow and continued to a quiet pool that was pleasantly cool.

There was something freeing about swimming naked, but when she rolled to her back, two interested males crouched at the edge of the pool.

Kresso cocked his head. "You know how to swim."

"I do. I love swimming."

He frowned. "You said you drowned."

"I did. The dam I was working on collapsed, and I was swept off with the rubble. The lake on the other side of the dam took me under, and even though I had jumped clear of the collapse, I was caught by some uprooted trees and held under no matter how much I fought. I saw my last breath floating away from me, and then I dreamed." She swam toward them. "And then I woke up, and a few hours later, I was introduced to your brother, and his scent was close, but it was wrong."

She pushed herself out of the water until her face was in front of his. "Your scent is much better."

He leaned forward and pressed his lips to her neck. "And yours is coming in fast."

She shivered and crossed her legs at her ankles.

"How did you choose if you can't determine scent?" Mahel asked from where he watched her.

"Oh, I can determine it. I can catch it. I know what I like, but it doesn't get to the point of me being insensible or out of my mind when the heat rises. It is like reading about a scent. It is identified, but it is grey and unremarkable. I know it can be so much more."

Mahel blinked. "You chose candidates based on that unremarkable translation."

"Yeah. Don't get me wrong. I still got hot, but again, it could have been more, and I know it, so we wait." She flexed her legs. "So, what the hell happened to you guys this morning? Claws, teeth, the extra necks." She raised her brows at Mahel. Kresso was still busy licking at her neck where her largest scent gland was.

Mahel grinned. "I guess you haven't seen an alpha ready to throw themselves into a rutting situation."

"Aw, sorry to disappoint." She smiled.

He grinned. "The linking isn't over, Lyra, and I am far from disappointed."

Kresso smiled against her neck. "It's getting stronger."

She looked away and pushed herself back into the pool, gliding easily into the deeper part before treading water.

Mahel stood, dove into the water, and disappeared. She looked around and watched under her for a flash of gold, but instead of pulling her under, hands slid up her body. Mahel wrapped his arms around her as he flew them both to a high peak with a lounge on it.

"This doesn't look right. Who would put a lounge on a volcano?" She babbled a little as Mahel set her down on the soft fabric.

"Imko and Himmy. Well, mainly Imko." He chucked and laid out next to her.

"It sounds like you know them fairly well."

He smiled. "Kresso and I were in the same training class. He went into medicine, and I entered the military. I spent a few festivals and holidays with their family; they spent some with mine."

"Well, that's nice." She turned and curled up against him, her fingers tracing his abs and trying to count. Her hand slowly moved down until she was circling his cock. She used a light grip that got firmer as she worked her hand up and down. He was hard, and precum started to leak the moment she touched him. She bent and dragged her tongue across the broad head. He tasted salty-sweet, and there was a musk that she had chosen from the different samples of scent. She pulled him into her mouth and enjoyed the heat. She pretended that there wasn't a fierce face on the other end of the body she was playing with.

She felt the throbbing of his pulse on her tongue and took him as deep as she could. She heard a strangled sound and kept going, up and down with her hands gripping his knot.

She felt him flexing, and then he lifted her away from him, muttering, "Definitely not enough, but a proper event can wait until we are—wait. Your scent came in."

Mahel flipped her to her back and dove between her thighs, his tongue sliding and slipping against her until it was inside and moving smoothly. She shrieked, arched, and twisted against him, but he held her with hands wrapped around her thighs. He reached with his thumb and stroked her clit, and she screamed as her body vibrated and her sex clutched at his tongue. He kept working her until she slowly dropped limply to the lounge.

Mahel raised his head and licked his lips. "You taste like nral berries now."

She raised her head limply. "Oh. Great."

He kissed her, and she tasted herself. *Holy crap, I do taste like the fruit.*

He pushed into her; she grunted and clenched around him. Lyra leaned up and licked at his neck. His scent struck her, she mewled and twisted when her arousal climbed, and she came around him without him moving. She whined, she writhed, and she began to understand why alphas wanted an omega in their bed. She wanted nothing more than to be with him, with him inside her at that very moment.

He gripped her hips and lifted her so that he was on his knees and she perched on his cock. He let her drop back in his arms and leaned down to kiss her while she circled her hips on him. She heard her voice moaning and whining and begging, and she didn't care.

She paused and shivered as she came.

He was amused. "Did you do that all yourself? Good omega."

She pressed her head to his chest. "Shut up, Mahel."

He laughed, so she bit his left pec, careful not to use her pointy fangs.

He slapped her butt, and she jolted and let his muscle go as she gasped. She felt the surge of moisture around him from the slap. She narrowed her eyes. "You know I can use Su'ath weapons, right?"

He chuckled. "I heard something about that. Imko warned me. You shot Kresso when you first saw him?"

"I did. Low-level stun blast. I caught his scent and saw the look in his eyes, and I shot him."

"What look in his eyes?" He grinned and rubbed a hand down her spine.

"The same look you have now, but now there are undertones to the scent I am taking in, and I appreciate it in a way I couldn't before."

"How do you feel about being responsible for bringing omegas back?"

She chuckled. "I didn't find out what the gestation for your people is."

"*Our* people. Himyana is in her eleventh month."

"Ouch. No wonder she's desperate to see her feet again."

He smiled. "The burden our females bear is great."

"Yeah, but guys like Imko giving backrubs is a mighty inducement."

Mahel smiled. "You will have two doting mates rubbing your back and your feet. And we will be there when our tiny girls are born, and we will raise them and protect them and beat the hell out of the males who try to get to them until they are ready and tell us it is time for us to let them go."

She kissed him as she absorbed the sweetest thing she could have imagined from this second life. She was dead, she was back, and she was going to have kids. Not bad for a fifty-eight-year-old hydrological engineer.

CHAPTER SIX

She was dozing on Mahel when Kresso joined them. Mahel pressed soft kisses to her cheek and stroked her hair while his purr rumbled under her.

"Her scent came in." Mahel smiled. She could hear it in his voice.

She knew she was covered in slick and Mahel's contribution, but she didn't care. She was purring softly and knew he was grinning.

"Our mate is a mess, Mahel." Kresso chuckled.

"She's relaxing into her instincts faster than I imagined." Mahel was smirking; she could feel it.

Kresso knelt in her line of sight and smiled. "How are you doing, Lyra?"

She smiled. "Nice. Good. How are you?"

"I am well. Sorry, I missed all the fun."

She gave him a sleepy look. "There is more fun."

He stroked her back. "Glad to hear it. Can you sit up so I can run some scans on you?"

She fought her pout. She never pouted. "I will get cold."

"I promise to warm you up if you get chilled. You are still changing, and we need to keep track of the changes. It will help the researchers if any of the others wake up."

Lyra sat up and scooted so her legs were over the edge of the lounge. Kresso had brought his kit with him and grinned. "You look relaxed."

Mahel chuckled. "I had to work hard to get that look on her face. Don't upset her, or she'll go after your cock. She could suck the plasma out of a grenade."

Lyra smiled at the surprised Kresso. "It makes him stop talking."

Kresso laughed. "Remind me to pick up an annoying habit."

He started the scan and frowned as he went past her belly and focused beneath her navel.

"Why are you frowning?"

He looked up at her. "How do you feel?"

"Fine. Sleepy, horny. Why?"

He chuckled. "You have something interesting going on."

"What?"

"You will be in heat tomorrow."

Mahel sat up. "What?" His shock rippled through the air.

"Yeah. You have an egg ready on the left and another on the right." He pressed a device to her outer thigh and checked a readout. "Your hormone levels are rising."

"Thanks, doc." She leaned forward and pressed her lips to his neck. "Any other words of wisdom?" She started to lick at his skin and breathe him in. Oh, this was much better than before. His scent moved along her skin, got into her lungs, and woke her body.

Her hand circled his erection and started to stroke. She looked up into his green eyes, and he exhaled softly. "I can probably stop."

He narrowed his eyes. "Don't you dare."

She chuckled and ran her fingers up and down the shaft with a snug grip. She couldn't wrap all the way around it, but part way was better than nothing.

His precum started to coat her hand, so she slicked it up and ran her newly slippery fingers up and down his shaft. His eyes were closed, and he was huffing slowly with her strokes.

He set his instruments down and slid two fingers into her as he leaned forward to tease her breasts with his tongue.

A few moments later, she was lying on her side. He had her left leg lifted and entered her sideways while she braced herself on the lounge. His thrusts took him deep and pushed her across the fabric. Mahel took her hands and gave her something to brace against. She gave herself over to the sensation and shrieked as Kresso hit the spot inside that Mahel hadn't found, and he had really been looking.

She bucked and shuddered as he kept stroking over it

continuously until she felt more heat inside her, and then he eased in until his knot was fully encased. He jolted, and she felt spurts of heat before he was completely wedged and immobile.

She looked at him, and his chest was gleaming and heaving with effort. Lyra squirmed, but he wasn't moving.

Kresso chuckled. "You aren't getting away, Lyra. I've got you."

Mahel grinned. "We've got you."

Lyra sighed. "What happens when I go into heat?"

Kresso leaned in and kissed her. "We take care of whatever you need, but we will have to mark you tonight."

Mahel frowned. "Why?"

"So that she can quicken with our offspring. Her body won't consider us suitable fathers for her offspring if we haven't marked her. Her body won't recognize us."

"Wait. I have a bouncer?"

Kresso frowned. "That word doesn't translate."

"A thug who waits at the door and ejects the unworthy." She chuckled.

He grinned. "An interesting image. Speaking of images. Don't you just look the picture of depravity speared on my cock."

She wrinkled her nose. "How could I possibly change the picture? I don't exactly have a tablet to read."

He lowered himself toward her and kissed her. "You know what is another delightful picture?"

She was wary. "What?"

"Your ears."

Lyra felt her eyes go wide as he leaned in and started licking her ears. She mewled and couldn't twist against him because she was immobile. She was pinned, and arousal was climbing, and there was no way to stop it. His tongue licked, sucked the tip of her ear, and ran around the edge of the shell of her ear. She tried to push at him, but Mahel held her arms, and she started to curse him out as she shuddered in a fleeting release as he kept going, and she kept clenching and fluttering around him while she whined that it wasn't fair around her begging for more.

Dimly she heard a voice say, "Kresso, we have gotten our mate all messy. What are we going to do about that?"

Kresso chuckled and stroked her back. "We will take her back to the house and bathe her, tend to her aches, make sure she is fed and rested. After that, we mark her and fuck all night."

She jolted at the last sentence. "Hey, it was all good up until the last sentence. I mean, that is good in another way, but you lulled me into a false sense of care and safety."

Kresso chuckled. "You will always be cared for and safe with us, and we will keep any other mates in line. And if we must part from you for any time, the other will watch over you."

She sighed and was gathered up against Kresso's chest as he got to his feet, and then they rose into the air off the volcano and in a slow descent toward the house.

"I don't think I am going to get used to this." She hid her face against his neck.

"What? Flying naked?"

"Just flying. It's freaky." She remained perfectly still.

"Twenty percent of alphas fly."

"And I am mated to two of them. Delightful." She grimaced.

"Oh, don't worry. We can do other things as well."

She opened her eyes, and he flew through the house to a central pool. He settled near the shower and turned it on, making sure it was warm before he stepped under the spray with her. He washed her with a strange move that made her freeze. His hand at her back supported her weight, and she was literally suspended by his palm.

"Is this one of those other things?"

He chuckled. "You are light as air, precious."

"I really don't think so, or you wouldn't say *oof* when I pounce on you. Oh, wait. That was Mahel. I will pounce on you later."

Kresso chuckled and finished rinsing off the traces of the afternoon frolic.

"Did I get a sunburn? It doesn't feel like it, but I have been rather distracted."

"Does your species suffer from solar exposure?"

"Yeah, we are radiation sensitive."

"We are not. Your skin is fine. Still pretty and silky smooth."

He held out his hand, and she floated from his palm to settle gently in the pool.

The pool was warm, and she relaxed instantly. Lyra paddled around and comfortably floated as she watched Mahel fly in and head to the shower. He rinsed off and turned to watch her in the pool. She lazily turned over, dove under, and then came up doing a hair flip worthy of a shampoo commercial.

She opened her eyes and grinned. She got them both. Her giggle was irrepressible.

Kresso wiped the water from his eyes. He looked at her with a narrowed gaze. "Accident?"

She shrugged. "Sure."

Mahel looked at her as if he was contemplating something and then sat on the edge of the pool, and without additional warning, he lunged at her.

She shrieked as his arms came around her, and he pulled her under the water. He kissed her, and she smacked his shoulders as her lungs demanded air. She finally went limp, and he pulled her up to the surface.

She sucked air in and started shaking. Mahel looked at her, cursed, lifted her out of the water, and held her in his arms.

Kresso got a medkit and scanned her. "What the hell. She's in shock."

Mahel winced. "I forgot that she drowned."

Kresso grabbed her head between his hands. "Lyra? Lyra!"

Mahel said, "I hope she doesn't hold a grudge."

The slap on her ass resounded in the room, but she inhaled deeply and punched Mahel in the chest. "Asshole!"

Kresso sat back on his heels. "Stress memory?"

"Yeah. Something was heavy on me, holding me down, and the air was running out." She looked at Kresso and jumped at him. He cuddled her, and she cried until her throat was raw and her eyes were puffy.

When she had finally slumped against him, he handed her to Mahel. "Now let him fix what he broke."

She sighed. "There is nothing to fix. It is a memory that is there when I sleep and again when I wake up. The hardest thing in this life was taking that first breath, not knowing if water and mud would rush in and if the world around me was an illusion." Lyra sighed again. "It was so hard."

Mahel cupped her cheek. "I am sorry. It is amazing that you survived your death. I will never play like that in the water again."

"Also, avoid mudholes. They might set me off, too. And stop smacking my ass!" She punched him, and he grunted.

He chuckled. "But you enjoy it on a basic level."

"Just because my body responds doesn't mean my brain likes it. If I ever request it specifically, feel free, but until then . . . No." She looked over at Kresso. "No to you, too."

He shrugged. "There are many other things that we can do, but I appreciate the clarification."

She nodded and leaned against Mahel. "I do like clarity."

She yawned and curled against him before she let a nap overtake her.

She was curled up in something soft and fluffy. Lyra stretched and wiggled her toes before sitting up. "Whoa." She was in a nest. A soft, fluffy nest made of silky fabrics and something that felt like fur. There was a border that fitted the curve of her back and was spongy but solid. She could push on it, and it bounced back.

She grabbed a loose throw and wrapped it around her, rolling and giggling. It felt so nice on her skin, and a tension in her chest that she didn't even realize she had been carrying loosened. She sighed and cuddled up in the different layers with one eye available for peeping at the doorway.

When she saw movement, she snuggled into the wall of the nest and looked through her tiny spy hole. Kresso looked at her and snorted. "You like the nest."

She stated, "Yes. It's comfortable."

He stood there and then asked, "May I come in?"

She nodded, and he stepped into the nest space, lay down, and settled against her.

He wrapped his arms around all of her layers, and she laughed. "Too warm!"

Kresso leaned back and peeled off the layers she had wrapped herself in. When he had reached her, he pulled her to him and wrapped himself around her.

She chuckled. "Still warm."

"Suffer," he ordered.

She laughed. "So, things are moving along pretty quickly?"

"Yes. It is remarkable. It is almost as if something or someone designed you to start replacing omegas."

She snorted. "You have seen my physiological makeup. I think that is what happened exactly. Why they needed my consciousness to run it is anyone's guess."

"You don't feel connected to your body?" He caressed her slowly.

"Nope. I am just watching the show. The closest to direct feeling was when I thought I was going to drown . . . again. That connected me to my body fairly quickly."

"What about the smack to your butt?"

"That caused a different response that I am not comfortable with. Not yet. When I want it, I will ask for it." She looked at him seriously.

"How old were you in your other life?"

She blushed. "I don't want to say."

He laughed. "Older that Himyana?"

She grimaced. "Older than her mother, probably Imko's, too."

Kresso laughed. "That explains that no-nonsense look in your gaze. Well, the soul is experienced, but the body is learning."

"Uh, the soul isn't experienced. I was what you would call asexual. No attraction for males or females, though I could appreciate a nice physique, I never wanted any part of it inside me." She looked up at him and made a face. "That particular urge is new."

He grinned. "I am glad that I am one of the targets of that urge."

"Where's the other one?"

"Atoning for his sins."

"What?"

"He still feels bad for putting you into that fight-or-flight situation."

"You twits are too big to fight, and pinned under you, flight isn't a possibility."

He nodded soberly. "You are very small."

"And yet, I am a standard-sized omega."

He wrinkled his nose. "It does feel slightly perverse to have this reaction to you, but instinct drives us, and I feel better having you in my arms."

"Better?"

"Relaxed, at ease. Happy, I suppose." He chuckled. "With your heat coming so quickly, there is also excitement there."

"How long does the heat last?"

He shrugged. "With the previous omegas, it could be up to a week. It stops when you are pregnant or when it runs its course. Four days used to be average."

She blinked. "Four. Days."

He kissed her forehead. "We will take care of you. You won't want for anything."

Lyra closed her eyes and felt the security of his body against hers. She realized, "But the marks first?"

He nodded. "The marks first."

"Oh."

He chuckled. "Dinner first. Mahel is cooking."

She blinked. "He can cook?"

"He can cook, play an instrument or several if I recall. He reads poetry and is a keen sportsman. He's also a masterful tactician and the pride of our fleet."

Mahel's voice came from the doorway. "Flattering? I would not have been as kind about you, Kresso."

She looked at him and smiled. "You are cooking?"

"It's ready to eat, but can I come in?"

"Sure." She held her hand out to him, and he crawled in,

settling against her back.

Mahel kissed her shoulder. "This is like being wrapped in an omega."

She chuckled and squirmed back against him.

"*With* an omega." Mahel nibbled at her shoulder.

She sniffed and bent her head to his. "You smell good."

"I have been cooking."

"No, this is different." Lyra turned her head and sniffed Kresso. "Oh, that's good, too."

She pressed her lips to his neck and started licking. When she gently bit him, he growled. "Okay, dinner quickly. She's losing control."

Mahel chuckled. "That sounds fun."

"Do you want her to remember being marked or just wake up in a few days with them on her?"

Mahel scowled. "Right. Up we get."

He left her and stood up.

Kresso eased her head away from his neck. He sat up and handed her to Mahel. She licked her teeth, still tasting him. Her fangs weren't down, so it was her incisors that had gotten a grip.

Mahel set her down on a chair at a dining table with five covered dishes waiting under a current of warm air. She shivered, and Kresso brought a throw from her nest and wrapped it around her, and Lyra smiled. "Thank you."

Mahel scowled. "Why is she cold? It's warm."

"Her blood pressure is not stable. A meal will help." Kresso sat.

Lyra picked up her eating sticks, and they were shaking so much that she set them down. "I am gonna get a fork."

Mahel took some of the fluffy starch, the meat, and a vegetable strip and held it to her mouth. "Here you go."

She took the first bite, mumbled thank you, and then Kresso had the next one. This did not bode well for the rest of the vacation. It seemed they had no trouble taking turns.

She didn't have a chance to say anything else. Whenever she finished one bite, there was another one waiting.

She held up her hands when she swallowed the last bite she

wanted. "Enough."

They were laughing. Kresso chuckled. "You can take a lot, Lyra."

She sipped at a glass of water. "Stop leering when you think that."

Mahel grinned. "So, how was the food?"

"Really good. I have no idea which vegetable does what yet. Can you teach me to cook?"

"Of course. Whenever we are here or on a world that has fresh food, I will teach you."

Lyra perked up. "We are going to other worlds?"

Kresso gave Mahel a serious look. "He will be. We don't know how fast your gestation will be, and if it is too rapid, you may have to remain grounded, Lyra."

She sighed. "Right. Small people."

"They are called babies, Lyra," Mahel chuckled.

"Ah. Right. Glad one of us knows." She sipped at her water. Kresso laughed.

She sighed. "Pity. I want to see the stars."

Mahel reached out and took her hand. "I will take you. We just have to work on the timing."

She nodded and smiled slightly.

Kresso asked, "Do your people trade with other species?"

"Nope. We are stuck on our world. No one around us as far as we know. It's quiet." She shrugged. "We are about seven hundred years behind MaKorith development. Two sexes. Male and female. They occasionally overlap but nothing like this species." She pointed at herself and them. "Sexual dimorphism is also prevalent."

Kresso blinked. "You just started talking like a professor."

She wrinkled her nose. "I used to lecture new arrivals at the dam. Sorry. I have a tone."

Mahel cocked his head. "I had a teacher with that tone. She was old and had the same kind of calm that you associate with meditation on a mountain."

She blushed. *Busted.*

Kresso chuckled. "How old are you, Mahel?"

He frowned. "Forty-eight. Same as you."

"Our mate is fifty-eight."

She smiled brightly. "And I look brand new."

Mahel's eyes gleamed. "You are older than we are?"

"Well, my mind is. I have no idea when this body was built." She shrugged.

Kresso nodded. "The research team is being very quiet about where the blanks came from."

"Why do folks keep calling them blanks? This is fairly well filled out." She looked down.

Kresso laughed, and Mahel explained, "The original blanks are generally shaped like you. The same size, same pale skin, but the arms are fused to the body, and the thighs are fused together. There are no features."

Lyra and Kresso looked at him.

He shrugged. "We found them twelve years ago and reported them to the government. We brought the blanks in and turned them over to the researchers. Twenty-four in total. You are part of the last batch from what my sources tell me."

Lyra blinked. "Huh. Do you know where they got the consciousness from?"

"We found some refracting equipment and brought that to the research team as well. I have no idea how they caught you, but I am glad they did." Mahel smiled.

She frowned. "But I died."

"And ended up in a living body, shaping it to your will."

"The blue hair, sure, but the purple eyes? Not even a little." She grimaced. "The body is familiar but shorter."

Mahel chuckled. "Travel-sized."

She snorted and giggled.

Kresso grinned. "I like that she is portable. Easy to fly with."

"Indeed." Mahel chuckled. "I have dessert. Back to the nest."

She tried to look for dessert, but Mahel winked and headed back to the kitchen.

Kresso picked her and her comfy blanket up and carried her back to the nest.

"Where is the large bedroom?"

"Other end of the hall. This was set up just for you." Kresso chuckled. "There hasn't been an omega here for quite a while."

"How will you know if I am pregnant?"

He gave her a droll look. "The old-fashioned way. Scanners."

She snorted and settled in with the blanket over her. "What did they do before scanners and bloodwork?"

"They would watch for the omega to start nesting. When you start stealing our clothing and weaving it into the nest, that would be a sign."

"Why would I do that?"

"The chemical signature we leave inside you will make you seek out our scent, and if we can't be there, our clothing can."

"Huh. Nesting in dirty laundry. Interesting. That wasn't covered in the history I have gotten to yet, either."

Mahel came in with a tray containing some dessert cream and fruit along with a sticky syrup.

She looked at it and got nervous.

Kresso caught the folded cloth that Mahel tossed to him. "Ease to the side, Lyra."

She scooted over, and he spread the cloth out. "We don't want to mess up your nest . . . yet."

He picked her up and set her squarely in the centre of the cloth. Mahel set the tray at the edge and climbed in. Apparently, like vampires, they only needed to be invited once.

Her blanket was removed, she was eased back, and a splat of dessert cream covered her navel. "What the hell?"

Mahel continued to dollop cream on her, and Kresso added the berries. Mahel said, "We are having dessert, and if you are good, we will share."

"What does *being good* entail?"

Mahel knelt back and cocked his head. "Don't spill the cream on the nest."

She watched as they did some sort of rock-paper-scissors, and Kresso leaned in to take his dessert off one breast. Her breath rushed out of her lungs, and he placed a berry between her lips before Mahel took his swipe at her lower belly. They took turns and fed her intermittently, but the cream began to melt, and they had to work faster as it dissolved in rivulets down her body. The backs of her knees were particularly sensitive, as were her inner elbows.

When she was clear of dessert, she breathed heavily, and her body was sticky. Kresso wiped her down with a grin and got rid of the sheet. When he finished, he looked at her, and she lunged at him with a feral growl. She took him to the nest and got him inside her, writhing wildly on top of him. He gripped her hips and rolled her beneath him, stroking slowly for about a minute until her frantic sounds and the pawing of her hands made him pin her, and he growled as he thrust hard until she felt the heat inside, and then he bit her on the right side of her neck, making an obvious mark that couldn't be missed.

His knot swelled, and he wedged it inside as his bite continued. Kresso freed a hand and worked it between them, rolling a fingertip around her swollen clit until she screamed, and he groaned.

Lyra was held, and when she came, her teeth told her what to do. She snapped forward and bit him on the shoulder. He hissed, and she felt more and more heat flowing into her. Whatever was in her bite was having an effect on her mate.

She whimpered as the heat kept building until she felt full. She kept her grip on him as another climax rippled through her, and he pushed even deeper into her. She finally let him go, and he groaned, releasing her and then licking at his bite. She did the same, but her bite had already closed.

He looked down at her, his chest heaving. "What was that?"

She chuckled and stroked his cheek. "Scan yourself and find out."

"I think I am fused to you." He chuckled.

Mahel growled. "You had better not be."

Lyra giggled. "I think I emptied him out." She winced. "Feels like it anyway. Is there a towel around? This is going to be embarrassing."

Mahel tossed a towel to Kresso, who put it under her hips. Two minutes later, he eased out of her, and the surge followed. Kresso sat back, and to her horror, he watched. He placed a hand over her belly and pressed gently. More trickled free.

"Sorry, Mahel, I have to do some scans."

Mahel growled and moved to support Lyra's head, lifting her into his arms so that her lower body was free for Kresso's instruments.

He scanned himself, he scanned her, and he sat there. "All male sperm are gone. There isn't one left. I knew what I was looking for, but I am still shocked."

Mahel nodded. "That is what we signed up for. Now, out of the way. I need to mark her."

"Make sure she can mark you."

Mahel chuckled and pulled her into his arms. She draped her arms around his neck and wrapped her legs around his hips. He settled her back gently to the nest and slid into her with a happy groan.

She chuckled and kissed his neck, jaw, and lips as they moved together until their huffing and thrusting were at the edge, and then he leaned back and sat on his heels while she slid over his knot, and he came when she did. The teeth sank into the other side of her neck a moment later, and she sobbed while her body throbbed around his.

Lyra waited until he stroked her clit to bring her with him again, and then she marked him on the right shoulder and hung on while he endlessly pumped into her. She groaned and let him go. "You are worse than Kresso." She ached but tended to the small marks.

He laughed, his teeth still in her neck, making sure her body recognized him for her heat and that her new scent was reserved for her mates or matching candidates.

He released her and licked at the marks while they waited. When he had done that, he kissed her, and she sat on his lap, fused to him while they waited for the knot to let her go. The kissing was sweet, and she lost track of time as they went from purposeful sex to lazily entwined.

When he started to come loose, he grabbed the towel that Kresso handed him with a grin. He tucked it under her, and the rush was caught when he lifted her away.

Kresso tidied her up and then curled up with her in the nest. Mahel joined them, and they slept together in a group while they occasionally tended to their individual marks.

By the time she woke, she was in heat and had pulled them along with her.

CHAPTER SEVEN

Lyra woke up in Mahel's arms, floating in the pool in the woods. Kresso had his kit nearby, and he looked exhausted.

She looked at Mahel, and he was in the same shape. "You look like a transport vehicle hit you."

He looked at her in shock and started laughing. "I feel like it. You have a lot of stamina, Lyra."

She smiled and yawned. "You gave me a bath?"

"Yes. You were showing all of our attentions. The bots are busy cleaning and rebuilding the nest."

She blinked. "It's over?"

"It's over. Well, this heat is over. If you didn't catch, there will be another."

Lyra looked at him and then at Kresso. "You guys need a nap. When will the bots be done?"

Kresso grunted. "In half an hour."

"Go sleep in the bed."

Mahel chuckled. "We tried. You would only sleep in the nest."

"Well, I am sober now, so go to bed."

Kresso looked at her. "You need to eat."

"I can feed myself."

They both growled. She wondered what the hell they had been doing with her while she was in heat, but it seemed that they were attached to her at the hip, so to speak.

Lyra sighed. "Fine. Feed me, and maybe the bots will be done by the time we finish."

Mahel smiled. "We can do that."

He walked out of the pool and down the path back to the house. Kresso followed with his kit.

They went to the kitchen, and she ate some fruit, cheese,

and crackers. The guys looked rough. She had a few aches and twinges, but in general, her body just felt smug.

She got up and said, "You two, wait here. I will be right back."

She went to the room where the nest was, and the bots were still busy. She grabbed a fuzzy throw and carried it with her. "Come on, guys. I have a portable nest if you two are on either side. Let's go. You look like shit."

They got up wearily, and she led them to the bedroom, pulled back the top sheet, and crawled into bed with the fuzzy throw under her. They thudded to the bed on either side of her, pulled the top sheet over them, and sandwiched her in place. They both groaned low and slept.

She chuckled silently and held onto them as they slept. Apparently, her heat was rougher on them than it was on her. Poor babies. She let their even breathing lull her into sleep. May as well. She wasn't going anywhere.

She woke when the next day dawned, and her mates looked rested. Lyra tried to get around them to use the restroom, but Kresso gripped her waist.

"Where are you going?"

"To the necessary. We have been asleep for a while."

He sighed. "Hurry back."

She grinned and went to do what she had to do. Her new biology had taken some getting used to, but now, it was all over and done in one disconcerting moment per day.

Tidying up was easy, and she washed her hands, then returned to the room and looked at the two men waiting for her with sleepy expressions.

"Hey, guys. Did you want to get something to eat?"

Mahel chuckled. "Later." He toppled her to the bed, nestling her between him and Kresso then stole a lingering kiss.

Her body melted, but her stomach growled as if on cue. That insatiable hunger was still there and quite noticeable now that her hormones seemed to be on more of an even keel. "No. Food now, sex later." She batted her eyelashes at Mahel. "I'm starving, and I know you can cook."

"Food it is then." He sighed and left the bed.

Kresso bundled her in a blanket, followed Mahel to the kitchen, sat at the table with her on his lap, and nuzzled her neck. "Your scent is enticing. I want to eat you up." He nipped her neck where he had marked her previously.

"The *food* smells enticing." Her voice sounded breathless, Kresso's teasing making her squirm.

Mahel set a plate filled with steaming vegetables and thinly sliced meat in front of her. He fed her a bite, and she closed her eyes and moaned. An assault on two fronts.

"This is so good." She took the fork from him and downed another bite.

Mahel dished up two more plates then joined them at the table, pushing one toward Kresso. They ate in companionable silence, surprising Lyra at how comfortable she had grown with her mates in such a short period of time. She had just started a second helping of food when Kresso's tablet began beeping.

"*Kresso. It's Himmy!*" Imko's voice sounded urgent. "*Her water broke.*"

"*Don't forget Lyra,*" Himmy's voice sounded strained in the background.

"She's early." Kresso swore under his breath, grabbed the tablet from the table, then tapped the screen. "Get her comfortable, Imko. We'll be there soon."

Lyra jumped from Kresso's lap and hurriedly dressed. By the time she had finished, her mates were waiting for her by the door.

Kresso slung his medical kit over his shoulder. "The transport will be too slow. We need to fly."

"I'll carry Lyra." Mahel snatched her by the waist, and they raced outside.

Before she knew it, they were flying high above the island and at a breathtaking speed. Her worry for Himmy and the baby was at the forefront of her mind. Ten minutes, maybe fifteen and she was being ushered into a building.

"She's in a lot of pain, and there is a lot of blood." Imko met them at the door and then led them to a bedroom. Lyra could see the worry etched in his features.

"How far apart are her contractions?" Kresso asked his brother.

"Five, maybe six minutes." Imko brushed a shaking hand through his hair. "I don't know. She's in a lot of pain."

Mahel drew Imko aside while she and Kresso approached the bed. Lyra knew Mahel was trying to calm Imko.

Himmy lay upon the bed, her face pale and contorted, her brow wet with sweat. Kresso brushed the hair from Himmy's forehead as if checking her temperature.

"Himmy, I need to examine you," Kresso told his sister-in-law. "You are going to feel some pressure." He pulled the blanket down that was covering her legs and lifted her gown.

Lyra tried not to gasp when she saw the amount of blood on the sheets. Himmy let out a scream, and her body bowed off the bed.

Lyra lunged to Himmy's side across from Imko. She leaned toward Himmy's ear and started to make a weird noise that her throat was creating on instinct. Himmy was moaning and panting, but Lyra kept crooning and rubbing her cheek against Himmy's.

Imko murmured, "What are you doing?"

Lyra shrugged while Kresso sat and checked the readouts.

"Bleeding is slowing, Himmy's body is relaxing, and the baby is ready for delivery. Lyra, keep that up."

Lyra kept the crooning going until Kresso delivered the baby and put it on Himmy's chest. Himmy laughed, Lyra's croon changed pitch, and she continued until Kresso grinned and nodded. "That's it. Himmy's out of danger."

Lyra stopped making the sound and staggered back, landing on her butt.

Mahel came around and lifted her to her feet. "Well done, Lyra."

"I am pretty sure Himmy did all the work."

Himmy and Imko were in a world of their own with their precious new arrival in their arms.

Kresso did more scans of Himmy's abdomen, and he was grinning.

"Well, sex is now authorized in six days or less."

Imko raised his head. "What?"

Himmy was enthralled with her new baby. "He said we can have sex again this week, Imko."

Imko blinked. "How? The other doctors said she would be wrecked until surgically repaired."

Kresso smiled gently. "She fixed herself."

"With a bit of help." Himmy grinned at Lyra.

Lyra stood back and looked at the infant. It was cute and super pink and kind of wrinkly. "What are you naming him?"

"Imarthen." Himmy kissed the baby's tiny cheek. "His name is Imarthen."

The umbilical had been cut at some point. Imko helped Himmy sit up, and they were smiling and cooing at their new arrival. Lyra leaned forward and flipped the sheet down.

She looked around. "Where are we?"

Mahel wrapped his arms around her. "Private wing of the capitol building."

Kresso cleaned his hands and finished packing his kit. "Better news. There doesn't seem to be any lasting damage to Himmy. I will need to verify, but she might be able to have more than the one child."

Imko chuckled. "Nice, but I don't care. I have Himmy safe. The baby is just a bonus."

Lyra smiled and relaxed. That had been nerve-racking.

Servants were called to help Himmy get dressed, and Imko held onto their baby while the relieved staff fussed over her.

After they finished assisting Himmy, they bathed the baby, dressed him, and swaddled him in a warm cotton blanket. Himmy gave the baby a dreamy smile when the servant placed him back in her arms.

Lyra looked at Kresso and Mahel. "How long do we stay?"

Himmy looked at her. "You don't want to stay?"

She was clean and in a soft gown that wrapped across the breasts. It was a sensible arrangement.

"I thought maybe you would like some time alone with your baby and your mate." Lyra knew *she* would after the kind of ordeal Himmy had just been through.

"We can always come back after you've had a chance to rest, Himmy," Kresso told his sister-in-law.

An alarm sounded in the building. Its high-pitched screeching tones made Lyra bristle.

"The building is being put on automatic lockdown." Imko snatched his tablet from the table and tapped the screen. "What is going on out there?"

Imko did not receive a response, and bars automatically came down in front of the windows.

Kresso peered out one of the windows and swore. "The alphas. There is a large group converging at the front entry. They must have scented Lyra."

Mahel and Lyra joined Kresso at the window. A crowd of large, muscular behemoths gathered at the front of the building, and the crowd was growing by the minute. One massive alpha flew in front of the window and grasped the bars, giving them a fanged grin.

Even through the thick glass, Lyra caught his scent. He didn't smell right. Lyra wrinkled her nose, stuck her tongue out at him, and blew him a raspberry.

Kresso chuckled and drew Lyra away from the window. "Do not taunt the alpha, Lyra. He might consider it foreplay."

"As if," she growled then bared her teeth at the offending alpha. "I don't like his scent."

"We need to get her out of here before she causes a riot." Mahel dropped the curtain, hiding the chaos outside.

"You think?" She put her hands on her hips and tapped her foot. "You gonna fly me out of here? Cause that might be a problem." She pointed to the other window. Two more of the alphas floated in front of it with leering grins. They didn't smell right either, so she hissed at them and hid behind Kresso's huge body.

"Use the sublevel emergency escape route. The tunnel will take you outside the city limits." Imko didn't seem concerned. He was engrossed in his mate and child. "There is a flyer you can use as well," he threw in.

"What about you, Himmy, and the baby?" Lyra gave Imko a sidelong glance. "Will you be safe?"

"They cannot get into the building while it is under lock-down," Imko assured her. "And once they no longer scent you, they will disperse."

"Well, that's good to know." She peered around Kresso and stared at the window. The alphas were still there, and another had joined them. Definitely not her type either. "Yeah? Well . . . I want one of those blasty things just in case."

"Blasty things?" Mahel asked.

"The Su'ath weapon she shot me with." Kresso chuckled. "We'll grab it on the way out, Lyra."

"Okay. Let's get out of here." Lyra wasn't in the mood to deal with a bunch of horny alphas, especially since they had the wrong scent. She was very happy with the two she had, thank you very much. She quickly hugged Himmy and caressed the baby's cheek. "We will visit soon."

"Yes, because I still want cuddles," Himmy smiled.

"Take her to your outpost, Mahel. It will be easier to keep the rest of the alphas away," Imko said as they left the room.

"Hold on tight, precious." Kresso swept Lyra in his arms, and he and Mahel made a beeline for the elevators, stopping only long enough for her to grab the Su'ath weapon.

She kept a tight grip on the weapon, hoping she would not have a reason to use it. Just as they stopped in front of the elevators, an alpha rounded the corner and stopped beside them. She recognized him as one of the guards that hand-cuffed her when she shot Kresso.

The alpha sniffed the air then grinned at her. "You look very cuddly." His eyes were on the weapon, and he drew in a deeper breath. "You smell delectable."

Her mates growled, and Kresso held her tighter.

"Down, boy," Lyra said when she was slammed with the alpha's scent. "Not interested." That seemed to calm Kresso and Mahel, but they still bared their teeth at the guard.

"Not even a little?" His shoulders slumped.

"Nope. Sorry. You don't smell right." She shook her head.

"I had hoped . . ." He heaved a sigh. "Anyway, you can't take the elevator. The system shut down due to the lockdown," he warned.

Mahel and Kresso grunted their thanks.

"Thank you," she called over Kresso's shoulder as her mates took off for the stairs.

Lyra was thankful Kresso carried her because the escape route was deep underground, and the tunnel was dark and damp. What felt like hours passed, and they finally reached the flyer and landing pad at the end of the tunnel.

Mahel readied the flyer, and Kresso seated his big body inside with her on his lap.

"We are far enough away from the capitol building that we shouldn't draw the other alphas' attention." Mahel slid into the seat beside Kresso and began pushing buttons.

"Stop at the island first. Lyra will need her clothing, and she needs to eat. It is a long flight to the outpost."

CHAPTER EIGHT

L yra yawned and burrowed deeper into the warmth of Kresso's chest. It felt like she was back in her nest. His scent surrounded her, teasing her senses. It made her feel protected. She felt secure in a way she hadn't known she needed. She'd fallen asleep in his arms not long after they had taken the flyer and headed to Mahel's outpost.

She cracked open her eyelids and peered through the forward window. The view was incredible. The dark, endless space surrounding them was filled with colourful nebulae, planets, and stars. Off in the distance, a large space station rotated slowly on an invisible axis. *I am in fucking outer space!*

"Is that the outpost?" Lyra stretched slightly, and her stomach began to rumble. No matter how much she ate, her body still insisted she needed more nourishment. "Is there food?"

"Yes, that is the outpost." Mahel grinned. "And, of course, there will be food."

Kresso gave Mahel a droll stare. "I am quite sure a feast has been prepared for your arrival." He dug into one of the bags they had packed and handed her a bright red fruit. "This should tide you over until we land."

Lira hadn't missed the sarcasm in Kresso's voice. "A feast? That sounds wonderful." She smiled brightly then took a bite of the fruit and savoured the burst of tart sweetness across her tongue.

Mahel sighed deeply, and Lyra could see him all but cringe. "If it is a feast you want, precious, then we shall have to make sure it happens." He leered at her, his eyes darkening with desire. "In private, of course."

The hot look Mahel shot her was enough to make her fangs extend, and she ached to take a bite out of her very sexy mate instead of the fruit still clutched in her hand.

Kresso inhaled deeply and grazed his teeth across the sensitive skin of her neck, making her squirm in his lap. Then he growled in her ear, "If you leave this flyer smelling as luscious as you do now, even the betas won't be able to control themselves."

"Then take care of me, Kresso." She twisted on his lap and flashed a smile to show her fangs had descended.

Her stomach growled again.

Loudly.

Lyra stared at the fruit in her hand then back at Kresso. Both were quite tempting. But . . . *Food first, sex later.* She shrugged and quickly took a bite of the fruit, the juices burst across her tongue, and she moaned. Yup.

Kresso gave her a calculated stare then kissed her. "Mmmm . . ." he said when he drew back. "A little tart, just like you."

"No time for play, Kresso. We'll be docking in less than ten minutes." Mahel pushed a button on the flyer's console. "Control, this is Captain Mahel. Prepare docking bay twelve for landing."

"*Aye, sir. Docking bay twelve outer doors opening in five . . . four . . . three . . . two . . . one. Docking bay twelve prepared for landing,*" a female voice responded.

"Thank you, Sergeant." Mahel disengaged the autopilot. "Coming in for landing."

"We'll finish this later." Kresso nipped the tip of her ear and squeezed her hip.

"Don't finish without me." Her teeth seemed to know playtime had been postponed.

Mahel grunted his agreement, swooped in, and captured her lips before releasing her and focusing on the landing controls.

Lyra's heart skipped a beat, and with the way her cheeks felt so tight, she knew she was grinning like a loon, but she couldn't help it. Mahel and Kresso made her feel . . .

Happy?

Yes, that's what she was feeling. It had to be.

Lyra couldn't remember a time that she had ever been truly happy, and even though she had been yanked from death and thrown into this crazy new world, her two mates were beginning to grow on her. It was more than just her body's reaction. She really liked Kresso and Mahel. A lot. She snuggled in Kresso's lap and took another bite of the fruit. By the time she finished the last bite of the snack, Mahel was guiding the flyer to a stop in the landing bay.

"Take Lyra to my quarters. I have a few things to deal with, and I'll meet you there." Mahel turned off the controls, opened the flyer door, and began to exit. Then his body went ramrod stiff, and he growled.

Lyra peered around his big body to see what had riled him up when the most enticing scent filled the air. It made *her* want to growl . . . and bite. She could feel her gums tingling and her fangs threatened to descend.

A group of three males and two females stood beside a small ship. They looked much like the MaKorith, but Lyra instinctively knew they were not. Their skin was tinged with red, and their scent was different. One of them smelled divine. She almost groaned out loud, and her body began to tremble.

The huge male in the centre of the group looked up and sniffed the air. His deep blue eyes met and held hers a moment before he mouthed *omega* and gave her a wolfish smile. His features were rugged, and the clothing he wore looked military in style. One of the females spoke to him and broke the spell. He then turned his gaze to Mahel and nodded curtly.

"What are the Su'ath doing here?" Kresso wrapped his arm around Lyra's waist, holding her against his body.

Lyra knew it was a protective move, so she leaned into him and let the warmth of his chest and spicy scent settle over her, calming her rattled nerves.

She looked again at the huge Su'ath male with a strong jaw and rugged features. He was a force barely contained, his muscles bulging with each movement. There was something about the male that made her want to crawl up that big, rugged body and take a bite out of him. Was it *his* scent that rattled her so? She couldn't be sure. She had trouble separating the scent threads, especially now that she was cocooned within Kresso's embrace.

"Who is the big one?" she asked, knowing that Mahel would know the face of his enemy. She sounded almost breathless, and her blood felt like lava flowing through her veins.

"That is Commander Ja'mor. He is rumoured to be their most skilled pilot." Mahel peered at Lyra, surprise in his expression as he caressed her cheek. "His presence is troublesome for us both, I see." He quickly turned to Kresso. "Take Lyra to my quarters. I will join you after I find out what these Su'ath want."

"Come on, precious." Kresso guided her away from Mahel.

"But Mahel . . ." she started, unsure why she felt the need to stay. Not for Mahel's safety. Her mate was strong and could defend himself against any enemy, including the ginormous Commander Ja'mor.

"Mahel will sort it out. It is safer for all concerned if you are tucked away in his quarters." Kresso urged her beyond the double doors to a long passageway.

She couldn't help but glance back. Her heart felt as if she were leaving a vital part of it in that landing bay.

No. Two parts. Her mind insisted because one of the Su'ath affected her in a way that only a mate should.

She sighed in relief when Mahel joined them in the apartment that Kresso had found by memory and scent. He had been at the outpost before.

Mahel seated himself beside Lyra and lifted her onto his lap an hour after she and Kresso left him in the landing bay.

"Commander Ja'mor informed me that the Su'ath found a lost research vessel, the *Cataclysm*, that belongs to us." He toyed with a strand of Lyra's hair before continuing. "The commander has been sent as an emissary to return the ship to us, though I think he may have ulterior motives."

"Oh, he has ulterior motives, all right." Kresso stopped pacing long enough to stare at Lyra and shake his head. "I think somehow that the Su'ath has found out about our omega research."

"I have no doubt that the commander suspects." Mahel caressed Lyra's cheek. "Especially now that he has seen Lyra, but the Su'ath are offering their hand in a truce. I have arranged for them to join us at the evening meal. I thought a more intimate meeting would be prudent under the circumstances."

"Do you think they can be trusted?" Kresso's expression was troubled. "Who is to say they do not try to kidnap Lyra? She is the only omega in existence."

Lyra cocked her head and gave Kresso a deadpan stare. "Then, you will make sure that I have my weapon close at dinner. I wouldn't want either of you hurt if things start to get a little bloody."

"So violent for an omega," Kresso chuckled.

"I need to be violent to keep the two of you in line." She gave him a smile and batted her eyes innocently.

"You might be the one that needs to be tamed." Mahel nuzzled her neck, his lips hot and wet, blazing a trail across her skin, causing her heart to beat a staccato rhythm.

Kresso knelt in front of her and parted her thighs, his fingers delving into her slick heat. When he leaned forward and captured her lips, she knew she was putty in their very capable hands.

"I'd *really* like to see you try," she whispered, surrendering her body to the exquisite feel of their touch.

Chuckles filled the air.

CHAPTER NINE

Lyra adjusted the shoulder straps of the pale blue gown she decided to wear that evening. Whimsical flowers embroidered in silver thread dripped from the V-necked bodice down to the fitted waist. Delicate silver sandals covered her tiny feet, and strapped to her thigh, easily accessible by a split in her flowing chiffon skirts, was the Su'ath weapon they had taken from Himmy's collection.

"You look stunning, Lyra." Kresso's green eyes held appreciation as his gaze travelled from her face to linger on her breasts then back up again.

"You smell incredibly luscious. And this dress . . ." Mahel brushed a wayward curl from her face. "You will make it very hard for an alpha to keep his libido in check," he growled then stole a kiss before taking her arm. "Come before we offend the Su'ath by being late."

"By all means, let's not offend the enemy." Lyra allowed her mates to guide her to the formal dining area. Three of the Su'ath had already arrived. The two females and one of the males. They were dressed formally in what looked to be military uniforms.

Mahel greeted them and then introduced Kresso and Lyra.

A tall female with yellow eyes and red hair stepped forward. "I am Captain Je'zera." She gestured to the other male and female. "These are Sergeants To'fel and Az'rea. Ambassador Ka'tar and Commander Ja'mor will be arriving shortly."

"I've never seen an omega before outside of a historical vid." Sergeant Az'rea stepped in front of Lyra, reached her hand out, almost touching Lyra's face, then dropped it when the deepthroated growls of Kresso and Mahel filled the silence.

"Down, boys," Lyra admonished. "This is supposed to be a peace meeting." Maybe the Su'ath weren't all thugs after all. Lyra took Az'rea's hand and touched it to her cheek. The female was quite beautiful, but even though she smelled nice, like crisp apples and warm cinnamon on a cold winter's day, it did nothing for Lyra except make her hungry. She grimaced when her stomach growled. "Sorry, you smell like apple pie."

The sergeant chuckled, her eyes twinkling with amusement. "This is a good thing, is it not?"

"If you were an apple pie, it would be." Lyra grinned and released the sergeant's hand then glanced at Je'zera's and To'fel's hopeful faces. Before she could say anything else, she caught a whiff of that delectable scent from the hanger, and all thoughts of food were lost in a haze of desire.

Nope, nope, nope, nope! Lyra closed her eyes and took several deep breaths through her mouth to squelch the fire that raged in her body. She refused to allow her hormones to interfere in such an important matter as peace talks.

When she finally dared to open her eyes again, Mahel and Kresso were greeting Ambassador Ka'tar and Commander Ja'mor. One of the two was the bearer of that scent, and she was determined not to let it get the better of her.

Mahel drew her forward. "Ambassador Ka'tar, Commander Ja'mor, may I introduce our mate, Lyra."

The ambassador took her hand, brushed his lips across her fingers, then gazed at her with wolfish eyes. "You are quite enchanting, my lady," he told her before releasing her hand.

His scent did nothing for her, and she could see the disappointment cross his features when he moved aside.

"Omega." Ja'mor stood in front of her now, his scent wrapping around her in enticing waves.

The commander was tall and brawny with red skin and rippling muscles. His long black hair fell around his shoulders in tiny braids, and his amber eyes danced with mirth. By the gods, she wanted to bite him; instead, she glared at him.

"My *name* is Yten Lyra."

"Yten Lyra . . . A beautiful name for such an exquisite creature." His voice was a deep growl that rumbled from his chest.

The way her name rolled off his tongue made her shiver, and when he lifted her hand and kissed her fingertips, an inferno ignited in her veins. She fought hard to hide her reaction. "Not a creature, an omega, a woman with two mates. But you have wit and charm inverse to your size. Nice body though."

"A-hem . . ." Mahel interrupted. "Why don't we be seated? The appetizer will be served shortly."

"Commander Ja'mor, you may sit next to me," Lyra announced. She peered at Mahel and Kresso. Both looked perplexed, but neither seemed averse to the idea that she was showing interest in Ja'mor. Good, because this Su'ath was hers, and she was keeping him. She looked to her mates. "He smells good. *Really good.*"

"You MaKorith have obviously been keeping secrets," Ambassador Ka'tar seated himself across from Lyra then took the glass of wine offered by one of the servers, and after taking a sip, he gestured to Lyra. "It is obvious you have stolen from us."

"I am not property to have been stolen from anyone, Ambassador," Lyra growled.

"Maybe not your spirit, Lyra, but the blank they used to create you was the property of my people," Ka'tar stated.

Lyra grimaced. "Not *just* your people."

"And the Su'ath have not developed the technology to bring souls into those blanks." Kresso stood behind her chair, his hand resting on her shoulder. "Lyra or any of the omegas that may survive the soul transfer are not property to be owned."

"How did Lyra come to be in your care?" Je'zera toyed with her wine glass, her expression closed. "The only known omega in existence. Surely the alphas of your species would not have allowed you to abscond with such a prize."

"Mahel and Kresso are mine, as I am theirs," Lyra stated vehemently. "*I* chose them to compete in the Omega Run based on their scent samples. They defeated a hundred other males and earned the right to be my mates."

"Then, Omega Lyra, if the MaKorith would like to continue our peace talks, you must have a Su'ath as well. I can arrange a competition between the alphas." Ka'tar gave her a sly smile. "Or we can dispense with the formalities, and you can mate with me."

"No. No competition, and I'm not mating with you." Lyra held Ka'tar's cool gaze.

"My people mu—"

"I have already decided." There was only one Su'ath Lyra wanted. She slid closer to Commander Ja'mor and let his scent tantalize her senses. "I will keep him."

Mahel chuckled. "Well, I guess that's settled."

Ja'mour slid his muscled arm around her, leaned in close to her ear, and whispered, "You will not regret your choice, little omega." A tremor racked her body when he nuzzled her neck.

"What of other omegas? You said others." The ambassador's voice pulled Lyra from her daze. "If we are to have peace, our people must be allowed to compete in future competitions."

"I am sure our president will allow that, but we will have to hold the Omega Run in a neutral location."

Ka'tar nodded. "That can be arranged."

Lyra nestled closer to Ja'mor and tried desperately to keep her hormones at bay while her mates discussed future peace arrangements with the Su'ath. It took the full dinner hour and a video conference with Imko to complete the arrangements.

Finally, after dessert and a round of wine, the Su'ath were leaving. Well, except for Ja'mor. And as soon as the room was cleared of all but her mates, Lyra jumped the burly Su'ath male and overbalanced him onto the table. She whimpered, squirmed, and his hand explored before she got his suit open and got him into her. She shuddered, moaned, and circled her hips while he was deep before she lunged forward and bit him, locking him into her family and ensuring more omegas.

He was startled, and her dress was pierced when he returned the bite. Deep inside, she felt him moving without his hips participating. Oh, right. Shapeshifter. Was this what they meant? Something was shifting, and it hit that sensitive spot over and over.

She groaned and licked his wound while he got her higher and higher until she shrieked as her body held him tight, and his knot swelled.

Somehow, they had made it to the bedroom where they began cautiously until Ja'mor, Kresso, and Mahel figured out their positions, and the tail end of her heat took them over.

Lyra dozed in Kresso's arms with her other mates around her. One appetite or another would wake her, and they would take care of her. In her other life, she would have imagined this scenario. She smiled.

She stifled a yawn and then shifted to look up at Ja'mor's face. "What's your planet like?"

"It is a beautiful place. Lush and green with many rivers and streams." He shifted, rifled through his clothing that had been strewn across the bed, retrieved a thin tablet, then handed it to Lyra after touching the screen several times. "This is my home."

Lyra gazed at the pictures in wonder. The city reminded her of images she had seen of ancient Babylon. The white-marbled homes nestled between huge gardens of flowers in many colours. Ivy dripped down balconies and pillars, and to her amazement, in the distance, an old stacked damn held sparkly blue water at bay.

"You'll have to take me to visit." That dam needed work, and she was just the engineer to bring it up to speed.

Ja'mor's eyes glowed. "We will have to take a vote. By the way, why did you bite me? I am not familiar with the thought of omegas with mating teeth."

"Well, I am the first of a new breed. Recycled omegas. Made from designs from at least four worlds with a soul from a fifth. I hope you are a fan of daughters."

"All omegas?"

"Of course."

He grinned. "Then, yes. Well, anyway, yes. I am excited at the thought of a family."

Lyra glanced at his cock and smiled. "I can see that. I need to know. The Su'ath are described as shapeshifters. What does that mean?"

He grinned and transformed into a wolf-style dog, as big as the man, with three eyes.

Lyra laughed and buried her face in his fur. She couldn't tell them, but she had a military man, free healthcare, and a dog. Even had three guys to boss around, which made her feel at home. Life was weird, but it was nearly perfect.

Authors' Notes

Viola Grace

So, this started as a brain worm, and I had fun getting it to Himmy's labour, but then I handed it off to Taryn because my brain broke. So, this has the potential to be one of six. If you want us to do it again, let us know on Facebook.

Taryn Jameson

I have read Viola's work from her first release and have always enjoyed her fun stories and twisted imagination, so you can bet when she offered me the chance to work with her on *Omega Run*, I jumped at the chance. I hope you enjoy our joint efforts! If you do, let us know. We'd love to complete the potential six books in the series.

ABOUT THE AUTHORS

Viola Grace (aka Zenina Masters) is a Canadian sci-fi/paranormal romance writer with ambitions to keep writing for the rest of her life. She specializes in short stories because the thrill of discovery, of all those firsts, is what keeps her writing.

An artist who enjoys a story that catches you up, whirls you around, and sets you down with a smile on your face is all she endeavours to be. She prefers to leave the drama to those who are better suited to it. She always goes for the cheap laugh.

In real life, she is now engaged in beekeeping, and her adventures can be found on the YouTube channel, Mystery Bees Apiary. Just look for the cartoon kittens.

Taryn Jameson is a mother, artist, and avid reader who lives in an enchanted forest that sparks her imagination to create. Her latest outlet is the written word. She is the alter ego of cover artist Angela Waters.

www.ingramcontent.com/pod-product-compliance
Lightning Source LLC
Chambersburg PA
CBHW070508130626
46555CB00003B/1201